Body Language

Posture | Head Motion | Facial Expression | Eye Contact | Gestures

Read What People Have In Their Minds

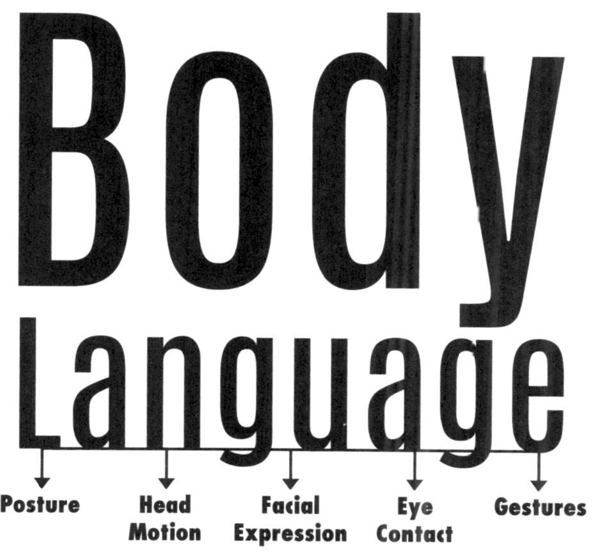

Read What People Have In Their Minds

M K MAZUMDAR

PRABHAT PRAKASHAN

Published by
PRABHAT PRAKASHAN PVT. LTD.
4/19 Asaf Ali Road,
New Delhi-110 002 (INDIA)
e-mail: prabhatbooks@gmail.com

ISBN 978-93-5562-774-2

BODY LANGUAGE: READ WHAT PEOPLE HAVE IN THEIR MINDS
by M K Mazumdar

Edition
First, 2024

Price
₹ 350 (Rupees Three Hundred Fifty Only)

Printed at
Sita Fine Arts, Delhi

Author's Note

Body language implies the language of the body, that is, the gestures and expressions that the body parts show. In our daily course of life, we express much without having said even a single word. This can be adjudged by the fact that our body expressions are able to make up the shortcoming of our words in a very simple and emphatic manner. According to the specialists of body language, a person expresses as much as seventy percent of his views through his bodily expressions. When bodily expressions are able to play such an important role in our lives, it is essential that we pay attention to our expressions as well as gestures.

What the body expresses can substitute thousands of words. Body language is much more effective than verbal expressions. Body expressions determine as to how a person will conduct himself.

An opinion about a person can be formed by the body language that are visible. If a person is able to understand what body expressions denote, he would be able to understand and know others better and he would be able to present himself in a better way; and this will bring about positive change in life. Body language is also being used to carve out ways to success, and it is also being used to improve upon personal relations with others.

The manner of conversation has remained fundamentally similar over the ages right since the prehistoric times; for example, shaking hands, nodding head, touching or tapping others' heads to console them, and the like. When we look at a person in his face, we are able to understand as much as half of the matter. Body language keeps emitting signals. It comprises a number of body movements, such as smiling, touching hair with fingers, holding ears, scratching ears, squeezing eyes, narrowing lips and the like.

Almost sixty percent of our conversation with somebody comprises of looking into the other's eyes with a smile. When you smile softly while talking nod the head, or shake the head you are taking interest in what the other person is saying, and it shows that you are trying to understand his thought.

Moving hands of a person during a conversation too has expressions behind the gesture. The level of your confidence is displayed how you enter the interview room how you sit in the chair, or how you talk. Your qualifications do matter but body language is given weightage.

Researches have revealed that women are able to understand body language far better than men. They smile more. Body language is like a code which is decoded by the other person before you. The more complicated you turn your body language, the more problem he would face to decode. The manner of your walking, moving and sitting displays how sensitive you are to the person you are interacting with or even what views you have about him.

If an endeavour is made to understand this language, we can transform ourselves into a more sensitive personality by which we can express ourselves more effectively. In the same way, we can understand the people who come in our contact by examining their body language and expressions in order to present our needs and views effectively.

—M.K. Mazumdar

Contents

1
Understanding Body Language

Body language is a language which reveals much without uttering a word in concrete form. It is considered to be the oldest language of the world. When human civilisation had not yet evolved, early man used signals or body expressions to express himself. These signals of the body are called body language. As mental development took place in man, he started understanding body language better. In the course of evolution, the first things to develop after bodily signals were words, which later transformed into sentences, and then evolved into language.

Presently, there are over ten million languages or dialects in the world. Many of these are on the verge of extinction because the number of speakers in them is diminishing. Owing to progress and development, some particular languages have come to dominate the modern way of life. This phenomenon has adversly impacted certain languages and dialects. Despite this fact, the first language of the world, that is, body language, has not been influenced by this phenomenon. This language being used all over the world.

The written history of body language is quite old. Its description can be found in ancient books of astronomy, physiognomy, body language, organ symptoms and the like. Despite this fact, most people did not know of this language until the ninth century. It was after this period that the focus of linguists was drawn to this language. They found that man, in addition to verbal language, utilizes his facial and bodily expressions in order to explain his point. The well-known Count Louis Heman, popularly known as Cheiro, has undertaken much research in this field. He wrote a book titled *Melosophy* which dealt with body symbols of human. This book became quite popular too. In this book, Cheiro has explained human nature and personality in detail. On the basis of which a person's face, physical constitution, voice, rate of speech and the like factors can be read. Cheiro not only analyzed every organ of man and woman, but also expounded theories on physical constitution and nature. This book took the world by storm. A number of its editions were sold like hot cakes. With this, people were acquainted with a new language. After this, this topic became a subject of serious study and research.

Meanwhile, a book titled *'Identification of Illnesses by Facial Constitution'* was published by Louis Kunai, the famous natural physician of Germany. This book took the medical world by storm. This book described how a person's nature and character could be identified by the shape of his face. It also discussed the unwellness which can be identified from facial constitution. When the modern scientists conducted research on the facts given in this book, they were amazed because these findings proved to be true after intensive and prolonged researches. Louis said that one cannot only know illness, but also disposition and character after seeing a person's face. The American doctor, V.D. Podolski says that body language can be used to identify a person's nature, behaviour, level and personality.

The Australian psychophysicist Allan Pease heard about body language for the first time in a seminar in

1971. When he thought more about it, a number of views arose in his mind. He started to discuss about them with his friends and relatives. He also studied more about it in the libraries. He noticed that only a few books described such a vital subject. At this, he compiled research findings of behaviourists as well as studies conducted in the fields of sociology, physiology, biology, education, psychology, family counselling, practical exchange and other subjects. He compiled the matter, and prepared his own book of body language. This was the first book which specifically talked about body language.

All over the world, people use their head, hands, body organs in an effective manner to communicate. T. Hall, an anthropologist, has claimed that as much as 60 percent of our interaction takes place through non-verbal cues. In such a situation, how can we establish contact with each other without verbal cues? Birdwhistle, a professor of psychology in Louis Ville University, says that body language has its impact like verbal expression. This effect is more effective than the performance rendered by a professional artist on the stage. The effect of body language is far more enduring than any words spoken.

When a pretty girl looks at a boy in a stylish manner, the boy cannot simply forget the gesture all his life. This style could not have been said by the girl verbally, and probably, the boy could not have been as much impressed had the girl used verbal expression for this purpose. Generally, people make use of signals or gestures in a very natural way; but they are little aware that they are using their body language in an instinctive or spontaneous manner.

There are number of gestures which are adopted by people in their daily life, like calling an autorickshaw by hand, showing red eyes to threaten, showing foot to disrespect somebody, showing fist to threaten somebody, tap the thigh to challenge somebody, attracting somebody by whistling, and the like. All these gestures are used by any common man knowingly or unknowingly.

Shaking hands is the initial form of making contact with somebody. It can help you know about somebody's nature, personality, impression, lifestyle and other things. When you feel the hardness or softness of his hand, you can also understand to some extent the type of work he does. Similarly, dirty or clean hands tell about his habits of cleanliness and lifestyle.

Besides the gestures of the hand, there are a number of facial gestures or expressions which play a vital role in expressing some point. The expressions taking place on the face tell about pleasure or sorrow, confusion or trouble, optimism or pessimism and the like. Similarly, the eyes speak a lot without needing any words to support them. This is perhaps the reason that the eyes are called the mirror of a character.

A finding in the research on body language has inferred that a person is able to tell something by his bodily movements and gestures what he could not have told by his verbal expressions. According to body language, a verbal expression by a person can be effective only when it is conjoined with physical gestures. This also means that there is more importance of how a thing is being said, than what is being said. According to a research, the impact of anything contributed by words is merely seven percent; while the remaining part is contributed by verbal cues, gestures, voice tone, facial expressions and the like. Specialists are of the view that silence is more vocal than words, so only it is advised that a person should endeavour to be natural.

Reading somebody's face is the work of a psychologist. But every other person cannot be a psychologist who could master the art of reading faces. Despite the fact that everybody cannot be a psychologist, everybody has some innate skill to identify others to some extent, which tells him about other person's nature or mood. This is quite simple to find out if the person confronting you is in good or bad mood.

When you focus your attention on the face, you can easily find out what is going on in his mind; his facial expressions will reveal much about him. Despite all the efforts, it is quite difficult, rather impossible, for anybody to restrain the facial expressions. The face comprises eyes, nose, lips, eyebrows, etc., but eyes have their unique place in the comity of facial organs. The eyes are capable of crying, raging, speaking, laughing and of course expressing love.

Some people are able to mingle with others in no time. It is due to the body language they employ. It teaches one how to speak when in the company of a particular person. You cannot mingle with a person or group unless you talk like him or them. It simply means to say that it is essential to conduct yourself as per the person you are interacting with. Sometimes, it might be necessary to affirm with somebody's contention even when you don't agree with him. Sometimes you might find the other person confused, but you have to bear with it.

When you say 'first impression is the last impression', there is psychology behind it. It is essential to understand this psychology, only then you will be able to present yourself before others in an effective manner. Psychological studies have revealed that if we fail to leave a good impression in the first meeting, it is hard to get positive response later.

Specialists suggest to keep one point in the mind at all times that the psychology of first impression is very important. When you are going to meet somebody for the first time, how can he form any opinion about you before meeting? If you are unable to leave a good impression on him in the first meeting, the other person might not like to meet you again. So, this is important that you bring out your positive points in the first impression itself, so that the other person is impressed by you.

Our dress is the repercussion of our etiquette, language and culture. The dress of a person is an important part not only of his psychological condition, but of his body language also. Dressing sense is very important to make body language effective because it enhances self-confidence. It does not entail that we should wear stylish clothes like film stars. It is advisable to wear clothes as per the time, place and environment.

Wit beautifies our personality and body language. When somebody is witty, it creates an impression by which the entire environment becomes memorable. When wit is conjoined with knowledge in sociology, recreation and general knowledge and other fields, then the environment becomes all the more interesting.

I was very much interested to read and know more about body language since my childhood. At that time, nobody could satisfy much of my curiosity. So, I adopted a method by which I tried to study the gestures, physical constitution and gait of a friend and then went on to discuss these features with the character. This was like a pastime and game then.

When I stepped out of my village to enter city life, I found a number of people who possessed the same interest in this field, but this interaction was limited to only discussion. Ever since, I continued to engage myself in its research on the personal level. Not much has been published on the subject of body language until now. There is much material available on the internet about it, but it is difficult to assimilate all that in a book of this size. Therefore, I have selected only as much information as should be essential for this book.

To write this book, I have sought help from a number of sources, including treatises, internet, conversation with people, idioms and phrases, etc. The information contained in this book rests on assumptions, and it is hard to prove it with specific cases of evidence. There might be cases when a particular piece of information may not fit on to particular person. Therefore, I would beg pardon on this score. I take this opportunity to state that this book has not been written to hurt somebody's feelings. This is meant only for information and knowledge. Body language is something which was used by our forefathers, and it has become a necessity today.

When you read this book, don't read it like a piece of fiction. Read one chapter at one time, think over it and then move to the next chapter. Don't guess about a person's personality only by a handshake. Don't form an assumption about anybody just by one feature and immediately on seeing him. It would be better to study a person minutely in respect of his facial expressions, gestures, gait, style of speaking, physical constitution and manner of handshake etc. Don't allow your thinking to be revealed for the heck of it. Just feel it within you.

□

2
Know by Physical Constitution

When a woman looks at a man with a fascinating, heart-throbbing manner, she is able to say everything without having to move her tongue even an iota.

All people in the world are distinct from all others. Physical constitution of a person is used to identify his nature and character. When we meet a person, the first thing that we see is his physical self before us. We notice whether he is infirm or strong, thin or obese, tall or short and the like.

According to the experts in body language, physical constitution of a person helps to know about a person. When you look at the physique of a person, you can know about his personality too.

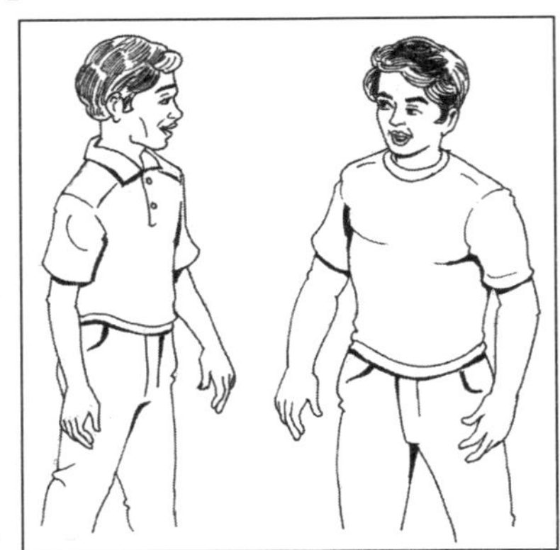

Weak and Thin Body

A person possessing a weak and thin body, small face, thin nose, pointed chin and pretty round face with a soft body is the one, who is mostly intelligent, simple in nature and witty. His mind functions swiftly. He responds to a query in no time. He is a little lazy and likes to meet few people, due to which he has few friends. He even behaves with his acquaintances quite dryly.

These people are included among intellectuals, they are apt in the art of speaking and conversing. They can speak fluently with any person. They possess abundant power of logic and inspection. They take interest in study.

Generally, this type of person is sensitive, spiritual and flexible. He is somewhat serious, idealist, principled and he also loves others. Such type of a person can be an oppressor, an envious person, an opportunist, and is repulsive to humans too.

Square Body

A person in this category has a body shaped like a square. The upper part of the forehead, jaw, shoulders, chest, hand and palms - all are square-shaped. His jaw bone protrudes near the eyes. His muscles are well-built and strong, his body is strong, he possesses a good height, and his hands and feet are pretty, strong and hard.

He is intelligent, emotional and sensitive by nature. Some people in this category prefer to use hands than the mind. They have interest in games. They like to join army or police and take up games like wrestling; they just don't like to undertake some sedentary work in an office.

Obese Body

A person with an obese body is a round-bodied man. His body is loose, short with inflated cheeks and wide chin. He has a protruding stomach, while his shoulders and chest are round. The people of this category are happy-go-lucky, skilled in behaviour, clever and intelligent. They take interest in light talks. They are fond of good food and good environment. As they are fond of eating, their body swells up to an unshapely size.

He is friendly but accepts challenges. When he has taken a challenge, he will stick to it whatever the outcome. He is seldom angry, but when he rages in anger, it is hard to control him.

If an obese person is short in height, then he is an ambitious, courageous, enterprising and powerful person. He is skilled in discussion. He does not retract in any debate. He can face any person fearlessly however strong or tall the person before him might be.

Weak, Thin and Short

A person falling in this category is hesitant, polite, soft-spoken and a man of few words. He is peaceful, simple and mild by nature. He does not like to mingle with others. Due to hesitation, he has few friends.

When he befriends a person, he abides by friendship lifelong. He easily gets agitated when some unbearable incident occurs in his life. Sometimes he is prone to lose his mental balance.

Short Height but Proper Ratio

A person with a short height but proper ratio of the body in terms of strength and form is more ambitious, enterprising, powerful and strenuous.

By nature he is fearless, independent and hardworking. He leads in discussion and debate too. He is engaged with his own things, but when somebody pokes him, he is not the one to spare him either. He is the one who responds with a greater might.

If it is difficult to attain something by the straight method. He doesn't hesitate to adopt wicked means too. He is a man of his own principles. He hardly likes the person who does not believe in his principles.

Due to short stature, he tolerates what others remark at him; but he also employs his wit and skill in speaking by replying adequately.

Strong Body but Short Stature

A person of this category has a strong and healthy body, but height is short. He is a witty, reasonable, logical, mingling and just person. How people can be quite unpredictable and might involve themselves in trivial matters. However, when they realize their folly, they repent it too.

This type of person can do some mischief too, but he is quick to beg sorry for his act when he realizes it. He is quite regular in work, and considers it sinful to violate any rule. He also feels bad when he sees others violating rules and regulations. He is ever ready to express his anguish at the person who violates the law. He never likes false propaganda, vainglory and falsehood. His heart is quite clean and pure.

Tall but Sturdy

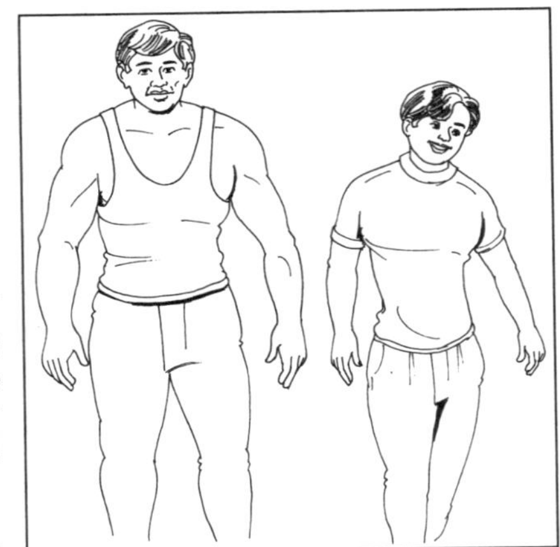

A person with a tall and heavy built is a person of serious nature. He does his work slowly, and while speaking, he thinks well before speaking. The tone of his speaking is slow and mild.

He is very proud of himself, and does not like to bow before others in order to get something done. He does not like to recommend others. He is quite emotional, even a tiny matter can hurt him greatly, and this thing can trouble him for long. It is difficult for him to forget his bad experiences.

However, he is not constant in his mood for long. He starts laughing in no time. He can change his mood unexpectedly. He can be peevish and unpredictable at different times. People flee from such individual, so he has few friends. However, once he takes somebody as his friend, he is ever ready to sacrifice everything for his friend, even to the peril of his life.

Huge Build

Some people are very huge and demonic, but a person of such a body is quite quiet, simple and mingling. He does everything after due thinking. He feels little anger, but when he feels unhappy. He is seldom ready to spare anybody.

He is not afraid of any problem. He confronts it bravely. He meets every trouble midway. He teaches a good lesson to any person who might be willing to suppress him.

A person of this category is quite hardworking and he is a workaholic. However, he is somewhat indolent who can keep off work. As he sits more, he becomes huge and obese, for which he repents later.

Long Torso but Small Legs

Some people have something unique of their body, the reason for which is the long torso but small legs. Such a person is witty and happy-go-lucky, due to which he is quite popular among his friends. He makes his friends laugh their hearts out due to his dialogues, actions and habits. Due to these factors, he has a large number of friends.

He is able to mingle with people in any company. He is quite distinct in any gathering or party. He is at once thronged by people. He is ever ready to confront the difficult situations of life.

His family life is generally successful. However, his wife often suspects him due to his witty and mingling nature, which can lead to misunderstanding, or even divorce.

Small Torso but Long Legs

Some people have long legs, in proportion to this feature, they have a short torso. Such a person is witty, mingling and entertaining. Whatever he does, he does with complete focus. He does not like to be lazy at work. He even warns a person who is lazy at work. He can point out even a person older than him or senior to him, including his boss, when he finds him slacking in his work.

He loves to do novel things and to visit new towns, cities and other countries. He loves to tour and travel. He works wholeheartedly in any adventure that he takes up.

He is volitional by nature. He does what he likes the best. He does not like to listen to others' commands. He is expert at work. He also loves to teach others, due to which his co-workers are normally unhappy with him.

Sturdy Body

A person with good stature and height, rising forehead, protruding chest, sturdy calves in legs, long back and straight body and by nature witty, selfless, merciful and determined.

He loves to contribute in public and social welfare projects. He is always on the lookout to find tasks which can be beneficial to others. He does not like to leave any task incomplete; whatever task he takes up, he accomplishes it completely, due to which he becomes a successful man in every profession.

He possesses unparalleled capability, swiftness, vigour, energy and enterprise. He doesn't leave work even when he is fatigued. However, repeated failure can make him peevish.

Pressed Head and Stooping Shoulders

When a person has a pressed head and stooping shoulders, he is normally jealous, discouraged, disappointed and mischievous. His nature is subject to suspicion by people.

Such a person commands more evil than good. Due to his these negative qualities, he keeps aloof from the society; people too like to keep off from him.

He does not do his work wholeheartedly and he seldom thinks before taking up a job. He is disappointed midway and stops it midway. Sometimes, he also gives up a task due to despair and negligence. His nature can be peevish at one time and quiet at another.

□

3
Know by Face

A person smiles when he is happy and his face glows. It has a simple scientific cause behind it. When a person is happy, his blood circulation improves, leading to a better flow of blood under the skin on the face, which helps the skin glow.

The face is the most important part of a human body. This is the part which features the character of a person. By looking at the face, you can in the first glance guess to which state a person belongs – West Bengal, Punjab, Tamil Nadu or Kashmir, and it also reveals his dialect or language and religion too. Looking at a child's face, you can guess who his parents are. This is the law of heredity that a child inherits his parents' traits, intelligence, stature and body. These characteristics undergo a change due to some irregularities during the course of pregnancy.

When somebody is caught red-handed doing something wrong, he hides his face with both hands. It simply implies that he feels shame for his act. The same thing happens when somebody tells a lie, he immediately covers his face. All these are instinctive reactions, which don't require a person to be told to react in a particular way.

For the purpose of body language, the types of faces have been categorized into different classes. This chapter will deal with how to identify a person on the basis of differences that different faces possess.

Charming Faces

Some faces are so fascinating that anybody is prone to think on looking at them: "If I were as charming as she!" Of course, charm remains the special quality of such a person. The thing to pay attention is that it is not at all necessary for a person possessing a charming face to have equally good qualities too. Such people have often been found egoistic. They have abundance of negative qualities like finding faults with everything, unpredictable behaviour, impolite comments and the like. They are also prone to have qualities like superiority complex, paying no attention to others, trying to prove their own side of the matter and the like.

A person possessing a charming face is fond of going about places. He is fond of meeting people too. However, he cares little for the people who do not agree with him; rather he may have some feelings of animosity against dissenting people. He is courageous and hardworking too. However, he cannot work for long because he lacks concentration. When you meet such a person, you have to be very careful and thoughtful while dealing with them because they can take offence for anything.

Happy Faces

Some faces are always glowing with happiness. Generally, they have an obese body, muscular face, short neck and flesh sticking out under the chin. Such a person has a large number of friends because his pleasant face draws anyone to him in no time. Women are generally attracted to such a person easily.

Whatever such a person does, he does well enough. His dressing sense, eating habits, gait are all quite unique, which reveals his happy life. But such a person also possesses certain negative qualities such as carelessness to work, self-appreciation, laziness, etc.

Ordinary Faces

An ordinary face has no specific characteristic to mark. A person with an ordinary face has no distinction, it is neither shabby nor attractive. Such a person leads an ordinary life. Such a person often lives his life without any specific goal. Rather we can say that such a person just passes the time of his life.

Every passing day for such a person is like a fleeting scenario, and he holds no hope for the day to dawn, nor does he possess any specific ambition. His life is somewhat like the sunrise and sunset, occurring at regular intervals without any particular change. He is a man of strong build, but he is unable to work very hard. He has no attraction for mingling with people, conversing with them or having ambition to accomplish great things.

Abnormal Faces

When you look at a person with a face that makes you feel something abnormal, he can be called a person with an abnormal face. Such a person may have a long or short nose, long or short ears, small or big eyes, small or cascading lips, big and unshapely teeth and the like.

Due to these abnormalities, such a person is often depressed, due to which he becomes peevish, angry and careless. He is prone to despair and disappointment too.

Your attention can be naturally drawn to such a person; however, he little likes people looking at him, due to which he becomes a victim of inferiority complex. The scholars of body language claim that such a person is the master of wonderful skills, but he little pays attention to them, due to which he fails in any enterprise that he takes up.

Extraordinary Faces

All great people in the world have possessed extraordinary faces. Their faces are different from ordinary faces. It is very difficult to compare or analyse them.

Tom Shell, who studied body language, says that the faces of important people including Subhash Chandra Bose, Mahatma Gandhi, Indira Gandhi and the like fall in the category of extraordinary faces. Such people possess a number of extraordinary qualities too. They are not at all ordinary to look at. This is the reason that their faces can be identified by themselves. They have few demerits, and if they have, they are concealed behind the veil of their good qualities.

Talented Faces

The face and personality of a person with a talented face is quite charming and attractive. He has an attractive and impressive language, gait and movement. If you look at Amitabh Bachchan, you can guess this point quite easily. His talent can be seen pervading his face. Such a person easily mingles with other people, he is simple, pleasant, intelligent and tolerant too.

Such a person is permeated with emotionality and imaginativeness. His high qualities include helping others, motivating people and cooperating with others. He feels happy when he sees somebody else making progress in life.

Work-oriented Faces

Square and rectangular faces fall in the category of work-oriented faces. They have squeezed cheeks, generally a small nose, small eyes and a sense of harshness on the face.

Such a person is hardworking; he likes to work hard and long. He likes to keep himself busy in work at all times. However, he is impatient in behaviour. He likes to help others. When somebody does evil to him, he does not like to spare the opponent.

Such a person attains a high place on the basis of his hard work. He never rests even when he has attained his goals in life. He continues to work hard all his life as he used to do during the initial phase of his life.

Emotional Faces

A person of such a face is pretty and possesses a delicate body. His hands and feet are quite soft and he is replete with womanly qualities to a great extent. He loves to be in the company of women. He is filled with wonderful intellectual abilities as well as emotional views, due to which he is able to cast a spell on others.

Such a person possesses an ordinary stature. Besides being hardworking, he executes his work carefully and beautifully. He is a sensitive person who can have tearful eyes when he looks at somebody's grief. He is ever ready to help others. He is generally devoted to his wife. Some of them have abundant womanly qualities, so they try to flee from marriage too.

Moral Faces

A person of a moral face has a long face, small eyes, long nose, broad forehead and curly hair. He is intelligent,

polite; he is efficient in good conduct and promotes new ideas.

His behaviour is very delicate. He talks quietly, he does not take tension. The high point of his life is that he has ambition to realize great things in life.

Due to his delicate and soft nature, such a person can be easily deceived by others too, which leads to failure in the enterprise. Despite this fact, he is seldom disappointed.

His smile is a source of pleasure for others. You cannot see his teeth when he laughs. Due to his laughing face, girls are often attracted to him easily. He also becomes a source of motivation for others due to his nature and activities.

Triangular Faces

Such a person has a broad face at the top while it tapers towards the chin. Due to this feature, his face appears to be triangular. If a person of such a face has glow and glory on the face with a bright forehead, he carries out appreciable tasks in life. He is intelligent and possesses leadership qualities.

He is determined and dependable. Such a person enjoys to do physical work. He is energetic. He accomplishes what he takes up. His quality of self-restraint keeps him normal even under difficult situations.

On the contrary, such a person can be selfish and quarrelsome, and can put others in a trouble. He seldom maintains cordial relations with his family members. He is quite confident of his work, but when he is faced with a trouble in his work, he blames others for his shortcoming in order to save his skin. He is never ready to accept his shortcomings and demerits. However, he never spares others when they commit a mistake.

Reverse Triangular Faces

A person with this type of face possesses sturdy and extensive jaws, broad cheek bone, small forehead with

small and close-by eyes, and the faces features like a reverse triangle.

Such a person endeavours to be happy at all times. His another greatest trait is his determination and energy. He is stronger and more powerful than others. He loves to undertake physical perseverance. His quality of self-restraint helps him keep normal even under difficult situations.

He loves to be patriot and disciplined, due to which you will find an abundance of such people in the army and police. His views are seldom conjective with others, so they remain somewhat aloof from others.

Such a person can possess a suspicious nature. As he doubts everybody, other people, including his family members and neighbours, are seldom happy with him. Even his wife is unhappy with him. Due to his suspicious nature, he fails to derive maximum advantage from his good qualities and capabilities.

Oval Faces

A person possessing a face like an egg falls in this category. His face is thin at the forehead, it thickens at the middle, and then it tapers down below, it makes a perfect oval face. You can commonly find such faces among women; men scarcely possess such a face.

A person with such a face is self-restrained, polite and kind. It is said that such a person is normally fortunate and he gets success by luck. Whatever project he takes up, he finds it moving progressively at a rapid pace.

A person with such a face is able to mould himself according to the prevailing circumstances. He is normally emotional and merciful, but he can be depressed due to his criticism. In place of blaming others for shortcomings, he likes to admit his shortcomings and accept the blame. He is often artistic in disposition.

He has a strong ambition to move ahead in life. When he succeeds at one phase, he sets out to conquer the next. He keeps himself busy in attaining higher goals all his life. His family life is happy.

Round Faces

A face falling under this category is the one that is round like a balloon, with abundant flesh and fat with sagging flesh. The entire face is round. The external circle formed by the sides of the forehead and ears appears like a ring. The width and length of the face is as good as equal.

A person with such a face possesses a pleasing personality. He is apt in talking and influences others with his talks. He has high fancies, and he builds castles in the air to fulfil them, because he seldom likes to work hard. He likes to laze about all the time. Of course, he is optimistic and mingles with friends easily. He is skilled in how to get things done from others.

He influences anybody with his sweet disposition and talks. He never runs away from offering free advice to others. He forgets about a person who does evil to him because he does not like to fight and quarrel. His behaviour is befitting. He can solve his problems with insight and ideas, but he cannot mould himself in every type of situations. He can also be boggled in emergencies.

Square Faces

This shape of a face looks like that of a square. The breadth of forehead and jaws is equal from top to bottom, and feels like a square. A person with such a face is practical in disposition, logical and rational, and does every work well.

It has often been seen that a person with this type of a face is truthful, reliable; and he does his work in a planned manner. He is emotional, sensitive and multidimensional by nature. He does not possess a sharp intellect, so he prefers to depend on his hands and feet than mind. He possesses a specific viewpoint in life, and does not change with time. He undertakes every task with confidence. He never flows with any convention. He carves his path himself. He behaves with others quite well. He respects all equally. He possesses a soft feeling for the younger. He always cooperates with his friends.

Long Faces

This type of face can be identified by its less width from side to side and more length from top to bottom. A person possessing this type of face pervades with intellect and number of other good qualities. He respects others, and his high point is that he accords love for the young.

Whatever task he takes up, he does it with perfection. He has a strong power of logic. He is always busy in learning and doing something new, due to which he accomplishes his goals on the basis of his own qualities.

If a long face is accompanied with fair complexion, such a person is attractive and pretty and possesses good qualities too. On the other hand, if a long face is accompanied with a dark complexion, such a person becomes unattractive, addict; believes in falsehood and shirks work. He also maintains relations with more than one woman.

Broad Faces

A person with a broad face has a broad forehead too. Such a person is farsighted, happy, tolerant, thoughtful and patient. Despite all these good qualities, he is prone to be excited easily. He also possesses demerits like anger and hurriedness.

Such a person can show different colours during the span of a short time. He cannot remain angry over a long period of time, he is pacified easily, but until then, much harm has already been caused.

He often bids to take credit for things. He pays more attention on the past things, and seldom cares for the future. He likes to work on new ideas.

Due to his hurrying nature, he often fails in his tasks, and then he sits down to repent. Despite this fact, he does not keep the past causes in the mind while beginning a new task. Of course, he blames himself for the past shortcomings.

Thin Faces

A person with a thin face possesses a small and infirm structure. Such a person is often ill, sorrowful and disappointed. His is peevish, lazy by nature, and speaks of his grief all the time. Whenever he meets another person, he starts to describe his travails, so people keep off from him.

On the other hand, if such a person possesses glow and reddish glory, then he is a scholarly and knowledgeable person who works in a better way. He is self-restraint, efficient in conduct and hardworking. He does everything with perseverance and attention.

The greatest demerit of such a person is his quarrelsome nature. He can quarrel with anybody even over trivial issues, without caring to know what its impact would be. So, he has to bear with harm due to this. Those who do not have this demerit, they are the people to fly to the unimaginable heights.

Small Faces

Such a person has all the facial organs small in size including nose, eyes and mouth. It is hard to understand such a person. According to specialists, he is often a person of deformed mentality, with no mental equilibrium. He often talks what has no relation with truth or reality from any angle.

He pervades with habits like telling lies, shirking work, forgetting work, laziness and the like. He is also inefficient in dealing with other people. He talks without head and tail, and he often uses a foul language. He does not listen to others carefully. He keeps talking his own mind, and is prone to spread rumours. He can quarrel with anybody without any valid reason too.

Due to physical infirmity, he is subject to others' sympathy, but his negative attitude keeps them away. He is opportunistic, and can even evade his family members.

Mixed Faces

A person with such a face has no specific norms. Due to varied shape and size of different organs of the face, they can be included under different categories.

Such a person has more good or bad qualities. If he is a person of good qualities, he has them in abundance. He is understanding and intellectual and can be compared with the best in the category. However, if he is a person of bad qualities, then no one can compete with him in them too.

Nature of Cheeks

A word has several implications; this thing equally applies to body language too. This feature applies to the time, situation and place. Raising the thumb means to seek lift in a vehicle in other countries, while in India, this gesture can simply mean to fool somebody or refuse something.

When we look at the face of a person, we first look at his cheeks. The area of cheeks is spread over the side whiskers to around the mouth and to the chin below. According to body language specialists, a person's nature, character and capability can be judged by looking at his cheeks.

Complexion of Cheeks

The complexion of cheeks can be white, rosy or dark. If the complexion is rosy, such a person has abundance of tolerance, self-respect, determination and self-confidence.

A person with red complexion of the cheeks is a person with a great innate power and energy. He is brave to the greatest extent. He is ever ready to confront the problems.

A person with pale cheeks is pessimistic, vigourless, cowardly, work shirker, who lags behind in life. Such a person has no normal life force, which is necessary for enterprise. As a result of this, his face looks disappointing and sorrowful. No specific hope can be expected from such people. Such a person is incapable to do anything, because he lacks courage. He often spends his life in some service. Such a person is also prone to illnesses.

A person with dark complexion is often sinful and selfish; he is unreliable as he says one thing and does another. Such a person is deceitful who often takes up unlawful jobs like that of a smuggler. He does not like honesty in life. He can be a thief or robber too.

Oily Cheeks

You will find some people with oily cheeks, as if they have been bathed in oil. This feature shows that such a person has a balanced energy within. He is more capable to take on challenges head on as compared to other people.

Such a person is emotional too, so he can take offence to anything, but he is also affectionate and can be brought to another viewpoint quite soon. He succeeds in business, so he is wealthy.

If oiliness of the cheeks is a bit too much, it shows that he is a luxurious man, with more enterprise, more vigour; he is also a swift worker. He shows no signs of laxity in his life.

A person who lacks oiliness on his face, or it is absent on his cheeks, such a person is very sentimental and dry by nature. His conversation is replete with indifference and egoistic disposition. He is a man of vainglory.

Very Dry Cheeks

The only mark of those who don't get nutritious food, who are inflicted with mental anxiety or depression or who have enmity for others is that they have very dry cheeks. You can find dryness clearly. They are peevish and bad-tempered, due to which they are prone to pick up quarrels at the drop of a hat. Such people find it hard to advance in life. They have more foes than friends.

Mixed Cheeks

Cheeks mixed with rosy and copper complexions are called mixed cheeks. While laughing, you will find dimples on these cheeks. Some people may have a dimple on the chin too. Such people are symbols of beauty, courage, soft-speech, lovingness and emotion; they are the favourite of all people. They also manifest attraction for the opposite sex, wealth and prosperity.

Round and Projecting Cheeks

A person with round and projecting cheeks are handsome and attractive. Such people think well before undertaking a task, only then they start it. Those with well-built and attractive cheeks are extremely ambitious. They are busy in grinding their own axe at all times. Those with extremely projecting cheeks are rather dull by intellectual level. They are habituated to work what others tell them to do.

Cheeks with Upper Projection

Those with cheeks tapering towards the top possess leadership traits. They are skilled in impressing others for getting their things done. They are light-minded, but at the same time, they can be equally staunch and angry too. They do not compromise with others. They abide by the principles they have once formed. Besides, they compel others to follow their principles as well.

Flat Cheeks

Those with cheeks which lack roundness, that is, with flat cheeks are hardworking. They greatly love to undertake challenging tasks. They are by nature harsh and dry, and are not good by behaviour. They have their own way of doing

things, due to which they seldom like somebody's advice. When they are in trouble, they don't like to seek others' assistance. They like to tackle their problems themselves.

Swelled Up Cheeks

Those with rosy swelled up cheeks possess a pretty and fascinating personality. Their personality is so fascinating that everybody is drawn to them by themselves; especially he is the focus of attention for the other sex. They are hardworking, skilled in conversation and thoughtful. They are mostly on high posts. They are also good in whatever profession they are, like business, art, politics or others.

Depressed Cheeks

Those people whose cheeks are neither projecting, nor round, they are described as having depressed cheeks. Such people work hard much, but they seldom achieve success. Their family life too sees many ups and downs. They live their life tackling the problems they continue to face.

Fleshless Cheeks

Those people whose cheeks have little flesh are often unfortunate, sorrowful and troubled. They always depend on others. However hard they may work, yet they are unable to get success in life. They find joy in doing petty jobs. Whoever comes across them, they start to count their sorrows, troubles and problems. If somebody chose to help them, they would just be after him.

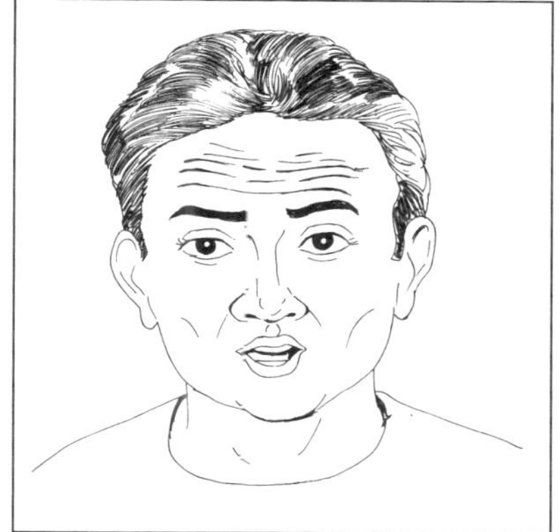

Broad Cheeks

Those with broad cheeks are quite skilled in their work. They are good at behaviour, civilized and patient. They mix well with others. They complete the task they undertake. They are never scared of taking up any enterprise. They have a high quality of self-confidence in themselves, on the basis of which they can take up any task upon themselves, and don't leave it undone.

□

4
Eyes Speak

The eyes are not meant only to see the world. It has a mute language too, which keeps expressing the innate feelings and emotions all the time. Truthfulness, sorrow or pleasure can be ascertained by looking at somebody's eyes. The thought processes can be easily identified by the movement of the eyes, especially any mental

imbroglio, despair, trouble and the like. The eyes reveal the emotions of pleasure, sorrow, meeting, departing, anger, hatred, love, psychosis, art, appreciation, character in both positive and negative shades.

This is the reason that the eyes are described as the mirror of thoughts and emotions. Edwin Selester, a well-known psychologist who studied the forms and types of eyes, has said that the eyes are the mirror of one's character. On the basis of behavioural goals of the eyes, you can find out everything about the personality of an individual.

If you want to know what is going inside somebody, just have a glance into his eyes, and they would reveal everything in distinctive ways. You will find the streams of love and flame of hatred. You will find the glow of attachment and signs of evil; you will find depths of love and shallowness of trickery. In the depth of the eyes are found several mysteries of love, which a lover can read on diving into them.

The experts in body language say that when two hearts meet, the pupils in the eyes show the depth of love and affection, and it is through them that love goes deep down into the heart. When a person is moved, his pupils spread four times more than ordinary. According to physiology, pupils are narrowed down in bright light. In dark, pupils spread out, and if this situation is blended with love. It leads to several times more intoxication, and it leads to transcendental feelings of love.

Men are rather poor in reading this unique language of the eyes, while women often can easily find out what is hidden behind the eyes and what type of man he is. Man adjusts his necktie and ruffles his hair and clothes in order to display himself when he is in the company of the fair sex, yet he finds himself unable to understand which woman is attracted to him and which is not. On the other hand, a woman has a number of tricks in her mind which make men mad after her. Her sharp glances and visual magic can turn any man into an ecstatic being.

A woman can reveal much without even saying a word, she uses just her eyes for this. She can virtually injure any heart with her side glances and low eyelids. Her eyes are permeated with attraction, style, mercy and love, and many other emotions, which she uses for a number of purposes. She can use her eyes like a weapon. She can use them to trap a man. She can pour love which can make any man follow her. She can create a sea of love, in which any man can drown. She can melt even the hardest man with the heat of affection in her eyes.

Men are often drowned in lake-like eyes because women reveal by their eyes that deep secrets are lying behind her eyes, which can be felt only by the lovers. The experts in body language opine that the spread out pupils show the depths of love. The truth remains that love enters the heart through the path of the eyes; it is a well-known secret.

Generally, lovers and couples are expert in reading body language by looking into the eyes of their partners. The lovers and couples who are unable to read body language remain sorrowful all their life.

When a person is excited, his pupils spread out four times than normal, and when he is angry or negative in attitude, his pupils are squeezed.

When a person looks into your eyes and says something, you can trust him easily. However, if he hides or deviates his glances here and there, it is the evidence of his falsehood. Such a behaviour can also be an outcome of lack of self-confidence too. If a person meets your eyes while talking, he is curious to know what effect he has on you, and whether you are listening to him attentively or not.

The shape and size of eyes of different people vary. Different positions and shape of the eyes can reveal a person's personality. A person possessing pretty white eyes is a person with peacefulness and soft heart; he is favourite, popular, thoughtful, just, talented, merciful, religious and clever. Those with dark spots below the eyes are lusty. Those with blue eyes are clever, lusty, intelligent, intense, serious and thoughtful. Those with pointed eyes are efficient in working.

The women walking with low eyes and the men walking with eyes to the top are introverts. Those who put their eyes into others while talking; that is, those who stare attentively and openly at others, are the people having command over a kind heart; they are honest, polite and dependable. A person who looks from the side glances while talking is the one who is selfish. A person who does not look straight into the eyes while talking, rather he steals his glances, he is a person of suspicious nature. A person with an evil nature is the man with ugly habits. If a person has his eyes close to each other, and who looks slantingly, he is not considered worthy of trust. Those who look from the side glances are the one who are detached with others, emotionless, goon and cruel.

Those people with the pupils projecting to the front are scholarly and open by nature. Those who close their eyes when they meet others' eyes, they are liars, cheaters, tricksters and evil-doers. Those who gaze at others all the time are stupid, violent and uncivilized.

Those people with big eyes and eyelids like that of a lion are just, unprejudiced and dedicated. A person with narrow eyes has a systematic way of life. A person with pale and impressive eyes like that of a tiger has the qualities of a tiger. A person with narrow eyes like that of a sheep is regular in his activities. Those with triangular eyes like that of a horse are hardworking. Those who have eyes like that of a snake, whose eyes appear to be floating on the sea, are often mischievous and aggressive. The people with small eyes like that of a monkey are unstable and troublesome.

Those with dark yellow or blue eyes possess a mysterious personality. Such people are not predictable, you cannot tell what they will do the next moment. Those with small eyes and pupils towards the bottom, like those of a bear, are cruel and wicked. Those with large pupils and small white portion, like that of a cock, are very courageous. Those with pupils like that of a fish, which are bent upwards or downwards, are unstable, lazy and infirm. Those with dark eyes are affectionate and liberal. Those with light brown eyes are sentimental, thrift and selfish. If the corner of the eyes goes down, it makes the eyes appear as if crying. If the eyes are bent down at the corners, a person is disappointed, despaired and indifferent to life.

Large Eyes

Large eyes symbolize prettiness. If the eyes are big, attention is drawn to them at first. This is the reason that women try to use make-up tricks in a bid to show their eyes bigger. A person reading the face should not pay much attention to the make-up, and should focus on the actual size and shape. A person with big eyes possesses open views, which can be understood easily.

Such a person reveals much about himself. It gives him contentment. A person with large and straight eyes is kind, merciful, clever, hardworking, thoughtful, efficient, enterprising, peace-loving and dexterous. He tries to mould himself according to the prevailing situations. A person with large eyes is honest and gentle, who easily mingles with others.

People trust such people, and want to share their matters with them. People with big eyes dislike those who want to conceal everything. They like to discuss everything in detail. Such people are active and imaginative by nature.

Small Eyes

You cannot simply measure eyes to know whether they are small or big. The size of the eyes should be assessed in the context of the entire face. A person with small eyes believes in secrecy. If he is open with you, he will tell everything that resides in his heart.

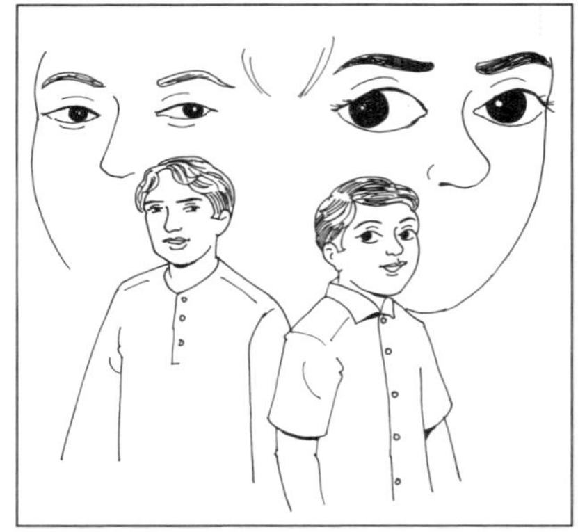

Such a person has a unique ability to focus attention at any one subject. He inspects and examines anything in its complete detail. However, if some work is difficult or monotonous, then he is repulsed from it too, and gives up the task in the middle.

A person with small eyes is often illiterate, illogical, extrovert and selfish. If a person with one eye small tends to close eyes while talking, he is wicked in the heart, though he displays himself in the garb of a perfect gentleman. Such a person tries to grind his axe anyhow.

A person with small, narrow but deep eyes is under the influence of the Saturn planet. He is serious, thoughtful, but suspicious, undependable, miserly. He possesses conventional views and is lazy. Mostly the gamblers have small eyes. The women with small eyes are envious, but they are volitional by nature. They are also clever, greedy and violent.

Projecting Eyes

The people with this type of eyes are vigorous and curious. They look for new possibilities in different areas. They love research and innovation. They like to peek into others' lives. They waste much of their time in interfering into others' affairs. They cannot stand by their promises for a long time. Due to this factor, they lose others' confidence.

Pleasing Eyes

Those with pretty eyes also possess a pretty personality. They possess love, affection, attachment, sensitivity, sentimentality and imaginativeness. Those with pretty eyes are skilled practical behaviour, intellectual, hardworking and social.

Such people take part in neighbourhood or social programmes; and if required, they spend money from their own too. As they take part in social work, they enjoy respect from others.

They are much attracted/intresting in to art, so they keep doing something for the sake of art. They themselves are artists, or they encourage other artists. Their married life is quite good, satisfying skilled in practical behaviour.

It is not necessary for all people with pleasing eyes to be pretty too. Some of them are very harsh, uncivilized and unsocial in terms of their behaviour; however, the number of such people is small.

Wandering Eyes

Those with unstable eyes are called people with wandering eyes. The character of such a person is not good. He is often selfish, trickster and cheater.

He is often involved in evil acts all his life, he is fully replete with evil. He is ready to do anything to lead a life of enjoyment and luxury. Such a person is also the one who has his heart on his palm. He likes to entangle girls in his net. He is able to impress others easily with his facial expressions and talks. Often the women are his victims.

Such people often pull girls by their acts, but as soon as they have met their selfish ends, they throw them out like the sucked mango, and soon they are on the lookout for the next victim. They cannot be trusted even when they promise because they are the ones who do not keep the word.

Such people can be better described as a snake in the grass. They don't hesitate to victimize even a person who has helped them. Due to bad habits, their lifestyle is poor, and their voice is harsh. They talk in a very negative manner. They love to use the foul language. The experts of body language recommend to keep away from such people. The psychologist Dr. William Tames says that a person can survive a snakebite, but it is hard for an unfortunate person to save himself from such people.

The women with wandering and narrow eyes are quite different by nature. They try to show themselves to be delicate and soft; but in fact, they are very harsh and cruel inside. They love their husband just to show off, but often have another on their mind. Such women are opportunistic; they deviate to whichever side appearing advantageous to them. It is hard to tell when they will trick you.

Tiny Eyes

The people with tiny eyes are normally introvert and talented. They mingle little with others. They keep away from discussion and debate. They talk in a fascinating manner, due to which they impress others; but they don't want to maintain contact with others, due to which they have few friends.

Their ambition is high, but their minds are filled with negative thinking, so they don't try to fulfil their ambitions. If they take one step ahead, they retract it at the next step. Such people are also unpredictable. It is hard to tell what they will do the next moment. By habit they don't tell a lie, but it is hard to tell which things they will talk at what time. They are unable to complete a task completely, because their minds are often fleeting.

Their eyes are attractive, due to which girls are drawn to them quickly, and try to come near them. However, these people are seldom interested in them. By the time they respond to a girl, it is already late.

Women with tiny eyes are very systematic and self-contented. They don't believe in a thing unless they have seen it themselves or have gathered all necessary facts. When a woman with tiny eyes loves somebody, she loves him all her life.

Round Eyes

The people with round eyes are extremely ambitious and wish to live a luxurious lifestyle. They are quiet, simple

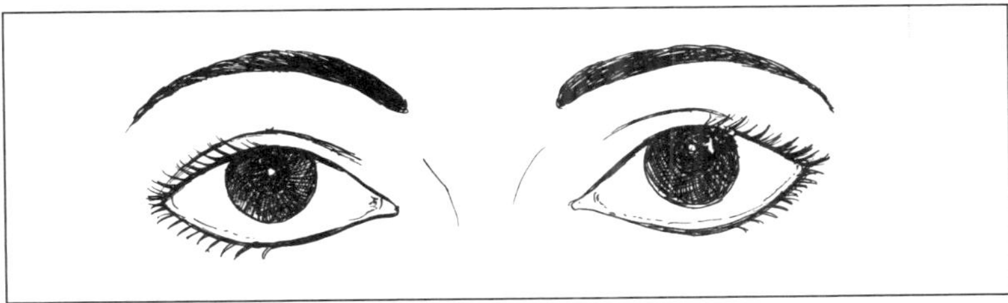

and pleasant by nature; but inside, they are quite opposite to these qualities.

They mingle with others, but try to serve their selfish ends at all times. They love tasty food, and they try to save every penny of their purse in case they can manage to get it without payment.

They wish to live life joyfully, but don't want to work for it, they want to achieve it at others' cost. They dream to realize their ambitions, but they don't work to achieve their dreams.

They talk of ideals, but they themselves keep away from them. They love addictions, drink wine; but they don't hesitate to tell in the same breath how bad drinking or smoking is.

Some people with round eyes have a quite different nature, due to which they are very popular too.

Broad Eyes

The people with broad eyes are quiet, happy and like to mingle with others. They like to help others and complete their tasks in time; they try to save themselves from evils. They are quite hardworking. They engage themselves in work. While working, they stick to their work, and they don't pay attention to other things at such a time.

On the contrary, a person with broader eyes is selfish, staunch, adamant and dull-minded. They are dependent on others. They don't complete their work in time. They trouble others by their actions.

If two broad-eyed people are together, it is difficult to keep them off. It is hard to tell how long they will keep happy or start fighting. On the contrary, if two broad-eyed people of opposite sexes are together, they remain very peaceful. They coordinate with each other. If two broad-eyed women are together, they run in different directions; they can't sit together for long, because soon they are involved in some hot debate or quarrel.

Downward Eyes

A person with eyes inclined downward has a strange disposition. He is habitual of criticizing others, finding faults with others, telling them good or bad things. He thinks himself better or the best, and he likes to steal others' credit.

He thinks many times over before starting a work, and can even refuse to accept a work at the eleventh hour. His nature is simpleton at one time, and quite smart at another. People coming into his contact are often bewildered what he actually wants.

During the day he is quiet, but at night, his disposition undergoes a change and becomes quite earnest. He often talks of disappointment, pessimism, impossibility and useless things. He is a talented person, but he is seldom able to control himself. He has the stair to success just at the next step, but he searches for it everywhere else.

The women with downward eyes are thoughtful, polite, simple and renouncing. They trust anybody, due to which they are often tricked.

Upward Eyes

Those with their eyes inclined upwards are merciful people; they are commonly players by occupation and patient by nature. They like to live in a peaceful environment. They like to remain happy and quiet. They are ever ready to help others.

They seldom get angry. However, if somebody troubles them, they cannot bear it. They have a large number of friends. When such friends meet, they encourage and invigorate each other. They like to talk to friends over a long period of time.

Their heart is always filled with anguish against injustice. When they see injustice being done to somebody, they cannot remain silent. They are little afraid of anything. They dislike liars and rumour-mongers, and keep them in the category of their foes of the second grade.

Circular Eyes

Those with circular eyes are expert in talking. They easily impress others with their logic. They examine everything in detail before setting out to do it. It brings them success in every field. They are farsighted and have a quality of thinking deep. They are clever by nature.

They win others' heart by their work and behaviour. They do any work very carefully. They do not like to be guided by others. Those who order them to do something are like enemies to them.

They don't allow anybody to know what is going on within them, even to the peril of their lives. They go deep down into any point. They take interest in spying or peeking into things, and of course, succeed too.

Remember, if a person has circular eyes completely like those of an owl, you can take it granted that he would be a person of quite a different nature. He would be selfish and trickster, so you should keep off from such a person.

Light Circular Eyes

Those with light circular eyes are selfish, attractive and impressive. Due to the attraction in their eyes, everybody is drawn towards. They befriend anyone quite easily and their friendship lasts long.

They are hardworking and are adept in their work. They possess profound imagination, and they fly into the realm of fancy all the time. Not only this, they endeavour to realize their dreams too, but they are disappointed quickly, due to which they fail also.

The people in this category are happy all the time, but they are not able to take advantage of their quality to attract others hence if they fail, they simply blame their luck and sit back silently.

Triangular Eyes

Those with triangular eyes are skilled in conversing, but they tell lies quite often. Exaggerating things, appreciating something purposelessly and self-adulation are essential parts of their personality.

They like those people who affirm what they approve, and those who don't agree with, they take them as their enemies. They go to the extent of harming them too. When they get hold of some tiny or trivial method to do so, they adopt it too. When they don't succeed, they look for some other trick to do so.

People with such eyes like to enter the fields of politics, sales or business. They seldom succeed when they enter other occupations.

Crescent Eyes

Such eyes are like the new moon on the second day. Such people are rarely found. They are dishonest, selfish and trickster. They like to accomplish a task only under pressure.

When they come to like something, they can go to any extent to achieve it. They treat those well from whom they have to get some advantage or favour. They are egoistic, and do not hesitate to flounder themselves even when they have little to display.

They can quarrel with anybody over anything under the sun. They are very brave in their own areas, but they are like the tailless dog in others' areas. It is difficult for them to forget something they have once set in their minds. Such people are strong in sexual urge, and can go to any extent for its realization.

Women don't like such people because they are the people of suspicious character. In some cases innocent woman can be befooled by them. If a woman ever comes into his contact, she is only cheated, and then she is left to nothing but repent at leisure.

Bright Eyes

When a happy person laughs, his bright eyes start to shine. These bright eyes further illuminate the personality; such people can be pointed out from a distance even.

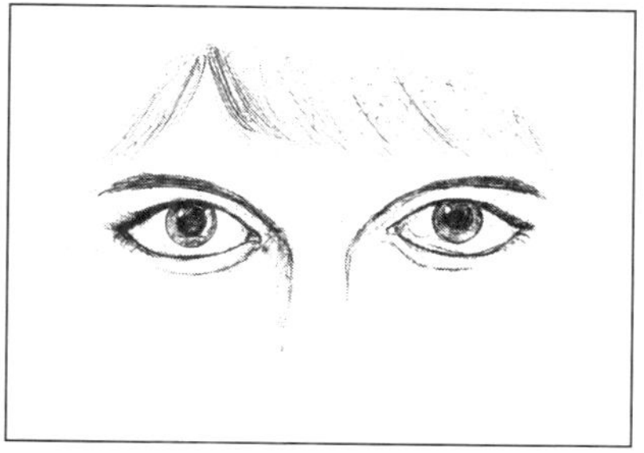

Their entire body is impressed by their bright eyes. People having this type of eyes have a clean personality, and are wordly wise. They speak clearly; they are patient and self-restrained, and they are punctual. Many people tend to follow such people as they are influenced by their behaviour, and try to emulate them into their lives.

Such people live all their life in a very systematic manner. Their family life is good. They have a large number of friends. Due to their nature, they get cooperation from their friends.

Depressed Eyes

People with such eyes are very negative in attitude. They have profound thinking and concern, but they are seldom able to utilize it in their lifetime, because they turn their deep thinking into negative thinking.

They are patient and stable by nature, and they take time to take any decision. They often change their decision at the eleventh hour. They don't share their difficulties with others. They hide them within their hearts. They only reveal their difficulties when some friend or relative asks specifically about them.

They are capable of influencing others, but the very next moment, they present their own difficulties, which eradicates their influence all of a sudden. They are skilled in talking, but are not expert to derive benefit from it.

Flat Eyes

People with flat eyes are always on the outlook for easy paths, due to which they often deviate from their right path, which makes their destination hard to achieve. As they keep changing their goals in life, success just bypasses them and they are unable to hold on to it.

They escape from struggle, so they can't achieve their destination which they ought to have achieved. They have their lives replete with irregularities, due to which they are unable to progress in their life.

Emotionless Eyes

People with such eyes appear as if they have been deceived deeply. They are quite pessimistic in their approach. This attitude is not due to their repeated failure, rather they declare themselves as failures, so they grope in dark.

If anybody tries to explain them something, they even draw him in their own viewpoint. If they do something they do with a negative attitude and if they fail they accept it as if they already knew about it.

They love a solitary way of life. They seldom like to meet people. They have a counted few friends. They don't like to share their hearts with their friends, or to seek their assistance. When they are immensely disappointed, they set out wandering or like to listen to music.

People with emotionless eyes are so desperate in life that they try to disclose their difficulties and problems before anyone, but they do little to solve their problems.

Reddish Eyes

Those with reddish eyes are people who are angry, cruel and unreliable by nature. Drug-addicts too have reddish eyes.

You should keep away from such people, but they are prone to do anything at any time as they lack self-control. People with red eyes are egoistic, vainglorious, angry, short-tempered, selfish, volitional, noisy and adamant.

One-eyed People

It is hard to know the nature of a one-eyed person. He is often a person with selfish, unreliable and wily attitude. He can go to any extent to serve his personal interests. He is often a trickster. If a woman is blind by the left eye, she is considered inauspicious. If a woman is blind by the right eye, she seldom enjoys the pleasure of offspring.

Blue-eyed People

A person with blue eyes likes to show off. He is abundant with cleverness, wiliness and wickedness. His actions are secret, and doesn't allow anybody to know what he is doing. He displays false gentlemanliness in order to trick others.

Women with blue eyes are intelligent, glorious, rational and vigorous. They don't do anything without due thinking. They don't retract even under difficult situations, rather they keep moving towards their goal under all circumstances. They love their husbands profoundly and are fully devoted to them. They hate falsehoods, but they like to be appreciated even when not true.

Brown-eyed People

Those with brown eyes are people of selfish disposition. They think of themselves and none else. They don't respect others' sentiments, nor do they care for social or moral obligations. They try to look into others' affairs in order to serve their selfish interests.

White-eyed People

People with white eyes are opportunistic. They can degrade themselves to any extent for the sake of serving their selfish interests. They are completely unreliable. They can trick anybody, including their family members and relatives.

Pale-eyed People

Such people are disappointed, desperate and lazy by nature. They accept themselves as inferior to others and present themselves in that manner. They are infirm by body and intellect. They are often suspicious of others, and possess a sick mentality. It is hard to make them understand anything.

The women who have pale, high eyes and who look through the glances have a doubtful character. Those who are involved in prostitution or taking advantage of their bodies have eyes like honey. Pale eyes symbolize a strong sexual urge.

Dusky Eyes

People with dusky or dusty eyes are not wordly wise and are opportunistic. It is hard to predict what evil they will commit at what moment. They are often indulged in intoxication or other evil habits, due to which they are engaged with themselves all the time.

Speckled or Spotty Eyes

It is as good as impossible to know such people correctly. They possess a mysterious personality. It is hard to guess about what they will do at any point of time. They have a sharp intellect, but they utilize it in doing negative things.

Green Eyes

Those with green eyes are nature-lovers and artists. They possess specific good qualities of kindness, mercy, gentlemanliness, practicality, sweetness, softness etc. They are always engaged in doing something new all the time. People with green eyes are very few in number.

Black-eyed People

People with black eyes are intelligent. They advance in any field they take up. They are attached to their work. They analyse any work well and then set out to complete it. They advance themselves, and help others to move ahead too. Their nature is quiet, simple and they are dextrous. They are liked by all people because of their good nature.

Rosy Eyes

People with rosy eyes are aesthetic people. They are deeply attached with nature, colours and arts. They are quiet, civilized, self-restraint and wealthy. They do their work very carefully and mindfully.

Rotating Eyes

People with rotating eyes are explorers by nature. Some of them could be mentally unstable; they can't fix their minds on any one thing for long. They sometimes engage

themselves in a number of projects simultaneously. Suppose if they have both a cup of tea and a glass of water before them, they may start drinking tea first, and when they think that it would be better to drink water first, they would keep down the cup and pick up the glass of water.

Gazing Eyes

Those who don't flap their eyelids and gaze intently at others are strong in sexual urge. They stare at pretty women and girls intently. Such people are uncivilized to a great extent. They don't keep off their bad habits even when they are in the company of their family members. They are sometimes thrashed due to their evil habits too, still they don't give up their negative attitude. People, especially women, should keep away from such people. It is hard to tell when these people can attack.

Flapping Eyes

Some people flap their eyelids continuously. They are often wicked people, but they present themselves as perfect gentleman. It is difficult to forecast their nature. They can trap with their sweet talks, but only to deceive later. They are shameless people. When somebody criticizes them, they only laugh it away. They are at the peak of their shamelessness when they go on to appreciate their evil achievements themselves.

□

5
Know by the Eyebrows

Before proceeding with eyebrows, let me tell you that those who twist their mustaches with one hand have a quiet nature; while those twisting it with both hands are harsh by nature. Such people try to impress others by twisting their mustaches.

Like eyes, nose and lips, eyebrows too tell much about the nature and personality of an individual. The face

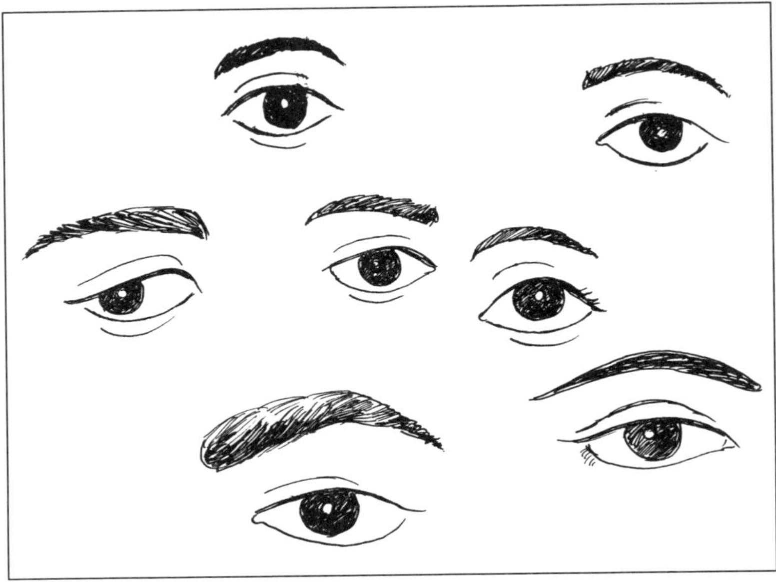

expresses emotions of mutual disharmony or opposition quite well. If a person has anger, animosity, opposition or disapproval for a friend or relative, his eyebrows will be depressed inside with a little squeeze. Both eyebrows too will tend to meet at the middle just above the nose where men daub the *tilak* or women put the *bindi*. Even otherwise, raising eyebrows is a popular idiom which means to get angry.

Small and Light Eyebrows

The people with short and light brows are people with suppressed or timid views. They are the ones who like to live a life of politeness, satisfaction, peacefulness and ordinary living. Such people treat all people coming into their contact in a friendly manner; they are soft-spoken and people of few words, but they are hardworking. They are quite thrifty in terms of eating, and they are pleased when they see their guests, and they welcome them heartily.

Thick Brows with Deep Hair

People with thick brows having deep hair are those who are proud of themselves and have a superiority complex. They like to impress others with their personality, and they assign their own work to others in order to enjoy themselves at leisure. Their sons and daughters like to keep off from them, the chief cause of which is that they keep pointing out shortcomings in them. Even their servants are tired of them.

These are profit-mongering people who like to earn more and more profit, as a consequence of which any customer is seldom ready to approach them again.

This is the reason that they fail in their business or occupation.

Brows Empty in the Middle

People with blank middle or with a few strands of hair in the eyebrows are the ones who have a clean heart. They speak clearly and speak the rational things. Such people explore the mysterious or divine elements, they treat others affectionately and possess significant knowledge. Such people are called talented, principled and farsighted.

Straight or Diagonal Brows

A person, whose eyebrows straighten at the nose and then bend down towards the ears, or go on straight, is the one who faces financial crunch and who succeeds in

his chosen field after a lot of hard work and a long wait. He has to face difficulties at every step. He also lacks vigour.

Such people undertake any task after due thinking, but they consider themselves a failure. They spend what all they earn. They hardly care for the future, and are fully engaged in meeting the present-day problems. The greatest demerit of such people is that they listen to everybody, but they do of their own and blame their luck.

Thin Crescent Eyebrows

A man or woman with thin crescent eyebrows is the one who is an addict, lives the life of luxury. He or she can be an artist or other luminary, and can impress others with his or her charm. Those who come in their contact are trapped in their honey. Such people are sharp-minded and prestigious people.

Joint Brows

Some people have a joint eyebrow, that is, the two sides of the eyebrows meet in the middle above the nose. Such a person is effecient in work, he also speaks in an indirect tone. Such a person does not follow the true path and favours the spouse.

Such people augment their contacts with other people to meet their selfish ends. If he possesses some skill, it is rendered useless. A woman with such eyebrows keeps her husband under her impression due to which she does not enjoy amicable relations with him. Even their parents are afraid of them.

They think themselves quite clever but they are prone to be deceived too. Such people aim at others, but only to be deceived themselves ultimately.

People with this symptom are not clean-hearted. They don't care for even family respect when it comes to money or marriage matters. It has been seen that the people with joint eyebrows have much hair on the body. Their gait is slow, voice low and plans long.

Thick and Straight Eyebrows

People with thick and straight eyebrows are people of angry disposition. They can thunder in rage at the most trivial things. They take joy when they put others in a trouble, they have no word like self-restraint in their dictionary. They always think of their own advantage. They can chase anybody for deriving benefit from him, and keep after them until their motive is realized, and as soon as it is done, then they disappear into thin air, and never tend to remember the person.

Crescent Eyebrows

People with crescent eyebrows are considered quite good, because they are quiet and soft by nature. They are art-lovers; they have a tendency to help others as well as have imaginativeness, due to which they are popular amongst people. They cannot bear with others' suffering, and they go to the extent of helping them in their distress.

Thin and Light Eyebrows

People with such eyebrows are clever, deceiver, work-shirker and indolent. They like to show off falsely. What they say seldom do, and what they do seldom say. They don't like to keep prolonged contact with anybody. They don't like to hear about their shortcomings, but they don't hesitate to count out others' shortcomings.

Thin and Joint Eyebrows

People with thin and joint eyebrows are quite restless and peevish. If something is delayed due to any reason, they become furious. They are habitual of criticizing others, propagating themselves, finding faults in others etc. They don't like to listen to their own shortcomings. If somebody happens to tell something negative of such people, they are sure to wreak vengeance on them, and seek pardon from them. Not only this, they impress the other person not to repeat such a thing in future too.

Short Eyebrows

Those with short eyes are hardworking; they speak little. They are contented and like to live an ordinary life. They are aggressive and restless. They want to get the desired thing at the drop of a hat. When they don't get something on time, they start to get peevish or angry. They can declare the entire world oppressor.

Eyebrows with Dense Hair

People with dense eyebrows are quite clever and dexterous. They are short-tempered and restless. They are unable to speak their heart out with anybody. They speak a lot of things in order to peek into others' lives. They look for selfish things in any and everything, and take interest in any task only when they find some advantage in it; such a task could be social, family or personal. They are atheist by nature.

If eyebrows are denser and darker than ordinary, they possess a pure heart. They are talented and serious. They use their pleasant views in order to brighten up the surrounding atmosphere.

Eyebrows Close to Eyes

People having eyebrows close to their eyes are wily, adamant and obsessive. They have high ambitions, and they can do everything to realize them. If the eyebrows are thick and dense near the eyes, it shows a furious personality. On the contrary, if the eyebrows are less dense, then they are the ones who spend their lives care with watchful decisions.

If a woman has thin eyebrows near the eyes, she has quite a disturbed life. If bone protrudes with such eyes, then she possesses ambitions more than their capability; and they are wont to disturb their things due to anxiety and restlessness.

Eyebrows Far from the Eyes

People with such eyes are artistic and aesthetic. They are attached to all types of arts. They possess good qualities, they are quiet and civilized, they mingle with others, and they are imaginative. They are able administrators and social reformers. They motivate others to keep off from evils and embrace good things of life. Their lifestyle is extremely refined. People like such people owing to their good habits and polite behaviour.

Distance between Eyebrows

If the distance between both eyebrows is uniform, such people possess an impressive personality. They are able to mould themselves under any circumstances. They motivate others to advance ahead. They help others as far as possible.

If the distance between the eyebrows is more than normal, then they have a harsh and selfish disposition, and don't hesitate to do even wrong things. More distance between eyebrows with less density shows intellectual capability. Such people are bookworms, they possess a higher intellectual level; they are very curious. They are out to explore one thing or the other at all times.

If eyebrows are very dense, it shows ego. They don't think any worth of anybody before themselves. A change in the quality and colour of hair can result into a change in their qualities too. When the strands of hair in the eyebrows are tough, they are furious by disposition.

Eyebrows Inclined Upwards

People with such eyebrows are the ones who possess high ambitions. Most of them are seated on high posts. They have abundance of leadership traits and power of logic. Those who are not occupying high posts are engaged in elite occupations. They possess a simple nature; they don't get angry easily.

Such people do their work in a planned manner. They may look careless from appearance, but they do their work on time. They teach the qualities of discipline, good conduct and punctuality to even the people associated with them. They live their life very joyfully.

Eyebrows Inclined Downwards

People with eyebrows inclined downwards are little educated and a little dull. They keep doing abnormal activities, due to which they themselves are troubled, and they trouble others too. If their brows are dense and dark, then their qualities are intensified. Such people are more thoughtful and are able to impress others with their work.

Triangular Eyebrows

Eyebrows with angular protrusion in the middle are called triangular eyebrows. People possessing such eyebrows are egoistic, adamant and vainglorious. They love to impress others with their influence, they keep praising themselves and they can stick to any point.

They don't flee from doing even wrong and improper things to meet their selfish ends. They make others do evil things too. They know well how to exploit others and how to take advantage of them. They are true lovers. If they love somebody, they love limitlessly. If the two edges of the brows are pointed, they are cruel and heartless.

□

6
Know by the Eyelids

Eyelids are located just above the eyes, they protect the eyes; they keep flapping over the eyes, it is a normal phenomenon which keeps occurring on its own. A healthy person flaps his eyelids as many as one hundred thousand times in a day. A person's personality can also be identified on the basis of distinctions by which eyelids are flapped.

Experts of body language are of the opinion that reading distinctions of the eyelids involves minute and careful study because flapping eyelids is a matter of a tiny part of a second. The number of flappings can be counted in order to understand the nature of a person.

Not Flapping Eyelids

When a person is shocked, his eyelids seem to have been frozen; that is, eyelids don't flap. Eyelids are also frozen for a while when somebody is frightened.

If a person thinks something deeply or earnestly, his eyelids stop flapping. Similarly, when somebody is lost in pleasant dreams, his eyelids don't flap.

Diminished Flapping of Eyelids

People whose eyelids flap slowly are poor, helpless and penurious. People inflicted with illness, amazement, flabbergast or trouble too have eyelids flapping slowly. The rate of flapping their eyelids is 0 to 5 seconds.

Flapping Eyelids with Some Delay

Those whose eyes flap with some interval in between, that is, they flap their eyelids once in 5 to 10 seconds are unfortunate and poor. They keep confronting troubles all their lives.

Normal Flapping of Eyelids

Those whose eyelids flap at regular intervals have a high intellectual level. Their conduct is simple and peaceful. They can understand anything quite easily. They are good thinkers and farsighted. They are engaged in their own purposes.

Frequent Flapping of Eyelids

Those who flap their eyelids frequently are people with unstable disposition. They are unable to focus their attention. Their heart is weak; they are scared all their lives. They are hesitant and are scared to put their point forward.

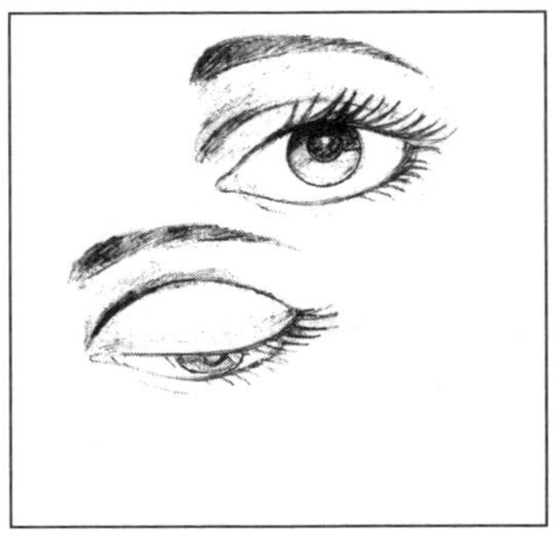

Heavy Eyelids

Those with heavy or thick eyelids are bewildered, confused, troubled and anxious people who are surrounded by irregularities of life. They are confronted with their own troubles all life. Their nature is peevish and dry.

Thin Eyelids

Those with thin eyelids are very fortunate. They are wealthy as well as happy.

Short Eyelids

Those with short eyelids are people with infirm and sick nature. Their disposition is quiet and tolerant. They are afraid to say their things before others.

Eyelids with Short Hair

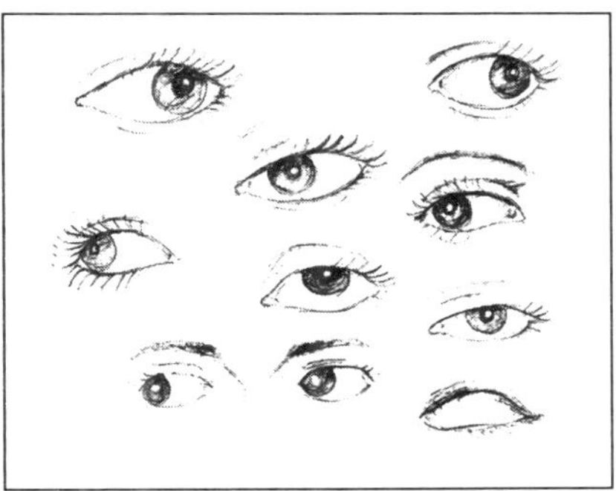

Those with eyelids having short hair are persons of a simple personality. They struggle in life, but are able to mould themselves as per the situation.

Eyelids with Long Hair

People with such eyelids are art-lovers or artists. They are simple, mingle easily with others and friendly people, equipped with all the good qualities. They are good lovers too.

□

7
Know by the Lips

Lips are very significant to identify a person by observing his body language. Shape, colour and smile of lips reveal a person's intellect, sentimentality, health and personality.

Dense Lips

These lips are large and muscular. People possessing them are happy by nature; they like to be busy in their own matters. They love to enjoy in light mood. If they are deprived of laughter in their life, they seem to have lost the rhythm of life and are rendered indolent.

Short Lips

Short lips are very thin, and when the mouth is shut, the breadth of the lips is equal to the breadth of the lower part of the nose.

Introvert people have lips like this. They love independence and they have a strong willpower. They are very attractive and hardworking, but they like to live a solitary life. Such people can be very lazy too, and it is quite a tough task to understand them.

Thin Lips

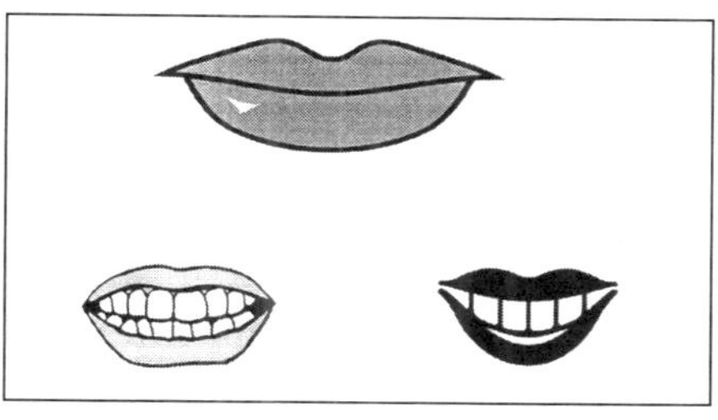

Hardworking and responsible people have thin lips. They work hard more than necessary in order to realize their goals, which leads to extensive fatigue, and therefore, they give up their objective in the middle. Often, they take life seriously. During stress, these people have a feeling of hardness and strange current in their eyes.

Straight Lips

Lips looking like a straight line manifest a person's intelligence and earnestness. Such people are good in conduct, soft-spoken and thrifty. Their special quality is that they like to help others.

If such lips are well-built, they are good artists who have carved a specific niche for themselves.

Thick Lips

Those who have thicker upper lips than the lower lips, they are often a good at communication. They are adept at speaking at every other topic. They influence others. They also try to suppress others including their favourites or near and dear ones. They can be deceptive and wily.

Large Lips

When the upper lip is larger than the lower lip, it shows mental anxieties. Such a person is surrounded by a number of difficulties. They have a high measure of endurance. They are also good at behaviour and work hard.

Short Lips

If the upper lip is smaller than the lower lip, it shows that a person is impatient and egoistic. Such a person also praises others for his selfish ends. They are seen to be work-shirkers too.

Sagging Lips

When the lower lip seems to be hanging down, it denotes that the person is contented and lives a regular and systematic life. He is engaged in his own matters; he helps others and it is in his habit to compromise in any matter. He feels pain when he sees somebody suffering. In such a situation, he helps him out even when he doesn't have resources to do so.

Rising Lips

Those with the upper lip rising upwards are somewhat greedy; they are after money whatever the trick they may have to employ; and they are engaged in this motive all the time. They can agree to do anything for the sake of money. They are fond of good food, and it is not that they would be ready to spend money out of their own pocket to quench their appetite.

Red Lips

Those with red lips have a good disposition. They denote an attractive personality. They are simple, hardworking and mingling type of people. They are happy in life and possess high ambitions; and they are able to realize their dreams rather easily.

Rosy Lips

Those with rosy lips are simple, attractive, tolerant and good at behaviour. They are very fascinating, especially the girls are easily drawn to them. Due to their grand personality, they are able to impress everybody who happens to come into their contact.

Dark Lips

A person with black or dark lips is involved in lies, trickery, wiliness and other wrong deeds. Instead of hard work, they like to advance in life through some soft means. Those with very dark lips are often addicted to some bad habit. Such people can also be suffering from ailments pertaining to stomach, heart and blood.

Blue Lips

People with bluish lips are not good at behaviour; they are greedy and selfish. They have no attachment in life. They are involved in serious addiction. Maybe they use snake venom as a drug. The number of people with this type of lips are rare.

Pale Lips

If the lips are pale or yellowish, it denotes the person suffering from an ailment concerning stomach, blood, kidney, etc. He is also found mentally infirm.

Oily Lips

Those with oily lips are somewhat mysterious. They show one thing and are another thing on the inside. It is difficult to identify them. A woman with oily lips is sexy, she can attract anyone with her attractive lips, but she does not allow him to impress her so easily.

Thin Lips

Those with thin lips are excited by nature, they can be excited in no time. They are also peevish, lazy and careless. It is in their blood to blame others for their own faults. They are always busy in finding faults with others.

Long Lips

Some people have long lips; this denotes lack of fortune and lack of wealth. Such people are quite irregular

and unsystematic. They are unable to do anything fixedly. They find it difficult to finish a project that they have undertaken and started, they accept their defeat midway; and then they start to do another thing midway.

Inclined Lips

Those with lips inclined to one side are greedy by nature, and they also suffer from some characteristic shortcoming. Given an opportunity, they lose no time in realizing their selfish goals. When they are in a trouble, they can do anything, including irrational and immoral things.

Parted Lips

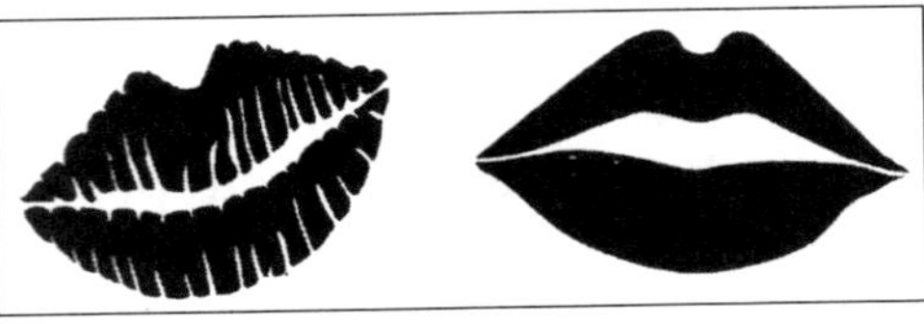

Those who have parted lips all the time, and their teeth can be seen, are luxurious, extravagant, addicts, unreliable and short in intellect.

Beak Lips

Those with lips like the beak of a bird are those who admire others falsely; they are selfish, unreasonable and impracticable, they speak a lot as well. They can be found surrounding at a place wherever they find some selfish ends to meet.

Oblique Lips

People with oblique lips are selfish with inclination towards falsehood and crime. They keep criticising others. It is hard to predict what they will do the next moment. A special feature of such type of people is that they can prove to be good spies.

Depressed Lips

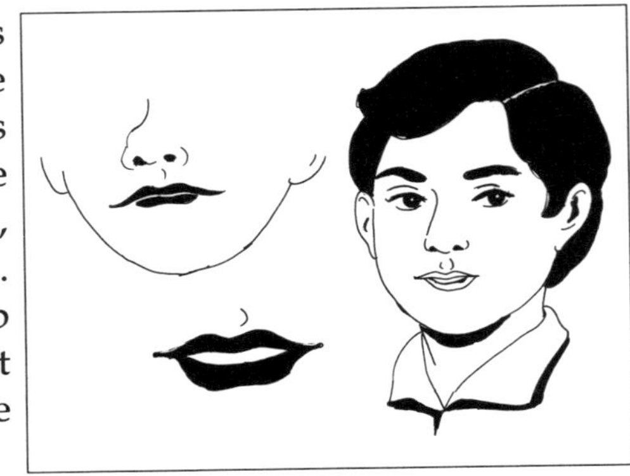

Those with lips depressed inside the mouth fall in this category. They are lazy, work-shirkers, unreliable and liars. They have a sharp intelligence, but employ it at the wrong place.

Very narrow Lips

When a person has very short and thin lips, he falls in this category. Such a person is egoistic and extrovert; he likes to sing verses in self-adulation. They don't like to hear any shortcoming or remark about them.

□

8
Know by the Smile

Smile manifests happiness, attachment, love and such positive emotions; but then, smile is also wicked which reveals a vainglorious personality as well as envy residing in the mind.

A research team in Britain undertook a long research in order to list different emotions found in man. This list included a total of 136 emotions and gestures of the face, mind and body. The largest number of these were those that pertained to the face or mind. This research team has ascertained some special types of smile, which help to know what is going inside man.

Ordinary Smile

Ordinary or normal smile does not show the teeth. It shows a light mood. It can be seen on the faces of those people who have no concern with what is going on outside. They don't take part in the world's activities. It is difficult to find what they are smiling at. Most of the time, they are smiling to themselves.

Medium Smile

In this type of smile, only the upper lip is revealed while the lower lip retains its place. This type of smile emerges

on the face when a person is in contact with somebody only by the eyes. Such type of smile is often used by a person when he meets his friends or when he is saluted by children. When children wish their parents, they normally limit themselves to a medium smile.

Those with a medium smile are somewhat reserved to themselves. They are busy in their own world and don't mingle much with others. They have few friends, but once they have formed friends, they can sacrifice anything for them. It is hard to understand what will make them happy or angry.

Broad Smile

Broad smile means to smile openly. This type of smile can be seen while playing or cutting jokes. It is not necessary for the eyes to come into contact with those of the other people. In broad smile, you can see both rows of the teeth.

If a person is laughing, it denotes that he is happy. Such a smile is often looked as a symbol of happy moments, but this fact is not true all the time and with everybody. A person can have a broad smile when he listens to a joke or interesting anecdote; but this type of smile can also be seen when some satire or abnormality occurs.

Lovely Smile

This smile can be better described as the one as possessed by the famous film stars Madhubala and Madhuri Dixit. When a girl looks at her beloved with affectionate eyes and a light smile, the beloved can have nothing in his heart but to take the girl in his embrace. This type of smile is an excellent weapon to get things done from others.

Fascinating Smile

Pressing lips under the teeth and smiling is called a fascinating smile. Often girls employ this type of smile to attract boys to themselves. It has often been seen that girls can cause heartburns with this type of smile, so it is also called a murderer's smile. This type of smile is also employed by wives to fascinate their husbands.

Struggling Smile

When the actual emotions are hidden with a smile, but in this the lips tremble as if struggling to maintain a semblance of smile, it falls in this category. Trembling lips, tearful eyes and reddish nose can reveal what lies within the heart inside. Such type of smile can be seen on the soldiers' faces who are now receiving the award for the travails of the battlefields they have gone through.

Rectangular Smile

In this type of smile, the upper and lower lips are drawn backward and they form the shape of a rectangle. At this time, the teeth are not visible. According to experts, it is advisable to keep away from such a smile, as it could be very dangerous. This type of smile can be seen on the faces of drunkards who might be looking to victimize a girl under some specific situation, especially when the girl is helpless before them.

Mysterious Smile

When a person has adorned a mysterious smile, it is hard to guess what he is smiling at. It is so mysterious that it is difficult to know whether he is happy or anxious or serious. In fact, this smile shows a variation between what is on the face and what is inside. This type of smile can be seen on the faces of those who are busy planning to defeat somebody in the game or trick. This type of smile is often found with those who are tricky, so this smile is also called Shakuni smile, after a wicked character in the Mahabharata. The smile on the face of Mona Lisa is also described to be mysterious.

Laughter

Laughter is an action which is undertaken by the mouth. A person can laugh in a number of ways. A person's personality can be gauged at on seeing the type of his laughter.

Laughing Openly

A person who laughs loudly and openly, he is liberal, kind, simple and clean-minded. Such a person takes everybody in the same sense, he does not distinguish between people, he is seldom scared of any problem and keeps laughing even when he is in a trouble. Such a person can be called a hearty person.

Horse Laugh

Some people laugh as if horses are neighing. They are actually hardworking, laborious people with a big thinking. Those who close their eyes while laughing this way, they are wily, clever, wicked and work-shirkers. They often take it negatively when others are being benefited. They can even try to harm such a person.

Loud Laugh

Those who laugh loudly are proud, hardworking and self-confident. Such people display a particular type of personality. They are busy carving a niche for themselves. Those who laugh at others or pass comments at others are egoistic, wily and selfish by nature. They are like chameleons who keep changing colours with the changing situations. It is difficult to tell when they will change their colour. They are ready to do anything for their selfish ends.

□

9

Know by the Nose

A nose can be long, short, narrow or pointed. The variety found in the nose is hard to find in other organs of the face. This makes the reading of the nose very necessary.

The Chinese are of the view that the nose is the measure to ascertain the extent of wealth, importance, intellect, learning and sexual urge. While reading the face, the shape and complexion of the nose should be kept in view; at the same time, the shape of the nostrils too should be kept in view.

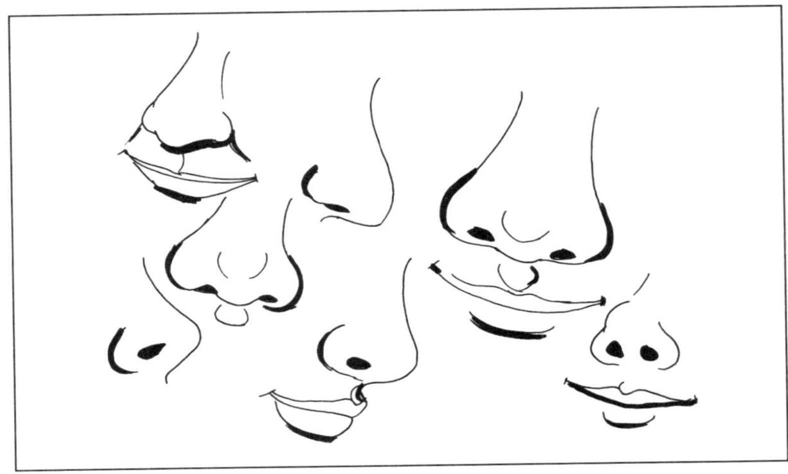

Flat Nose

Those with a broad or flat nose have interests in a number of fields, whether they are in social, political or environmental fields. They are happy and social people. A shortcoming in them is that they are unable to take major decisions for themselves. They are able to mingle with others in no time. They prove to be good friends as well as lovers.

Short and Narrow Nose

People with such a nose know well how to keep their sentiments under control. Though these people can be hesitant at any public function or opportunity, yet they have a great capability to remain neutral. They don't like much of laughter, jokes and light-hearted comments. They believe in truth and actual affairs. They cannot waste time, and take care of their money.

Large Nose

If you find the nose to be the most prominent part of a face, you can easily call him a large-nosed man. Such people pass through sentimentality all their lives. They are motivated people and keep ahead of their competitors in their respective fields. A person with a large nose is intelligent, honest and hardworking. He enjoys his work immensely.

Straight Nose

Those with a straight nose are impressive and attractive to look at. They are reliable, patient and self-restraint, and possess good thoughts. Most of such people carve a special place for themselves. They are good speakers; they take much interest in spirituality and religion. They sacrifice their lives for this goal.

Long Nose

Those with a long nose are efficient workers, self-confident, serious; they have faith in religion and rituals. They have much interest in the arts, which can lead them to become great artists. They are dexterous and active by nature. If the nose is long but thin, they can be peevish and egoistic. If the long nose is also broad, it shows self-ego by nature.

Sharp Nose

A person with a sharp nose is peevish, clever, wily, cruel and wicked. He can be perturbed by anything any moment. He is unable to digest any information; he is proud of himself.

Due to their habits, few people like them. If somebody happens to praise them, they think it their greatest merit. Those with a little oblique but sharp nose are unreliable by nature. They can deceive anybody.

High Nose

Those with a nose turning upwards are wanderers, spendthrifts and volitional. As they have interest in going places, they have a good level of general knowledge. They have a large number of friends and they can make friends easily.

They are always on a spending spree. They can spend even the last paisa in their pockets. Their married life is not good, they are not at good relations with their wives. If both husband and wife have upturned noses, they may go to the extent of divorce.

Mature Nose

A large, broad nose that is sharp at the front is called a mature nose. A person with such a nose has interest in arts and artists. He himself is a good artist. He is very intelligent, polite, civilized and mingles with others, due to which he gets respect from everybody. He lives his life happily and in abundance.

Immature Nose

A small, flat and insignificant nose falls in the category of an immature nose. Such a person is miserly, peevish and unable to work hard. His family life is full of strife. His conduct is not good. He does not take joy in mingling with people.

Undeveloped Nose

A small nose which is turned at the top falls in this category. Those with an undeveloped nose have a low level of intellect. He is neither able to understand things well, nor can he explain things to others. He is attached to old things. They have interest in doing a petty business like dealing in old things. However, he finds it difficult to manage things even in small businesses, due to which he fails quite often.

Hooked Nose

Those with a nose like a hook live a life of luxury and wealth. They stick to their word; they fulfil what they have said once. They are always engaged in their own matter. They can earn profits with their intellect and reason. They have much interest in material comforts and luxury.

Narrow Nose

A nose that tapers from top to bottom falls in this category. A person with such a nose is selfish, and is always running after realizing his selfish interests. Before taking up a project, he looks for any advantage that he might derive from it. If he sees no advantage to himself, he will be unwilling to undertake it. Given an opportunity, he can deceive anybody. He can deceive even his own people when their own interests are clashing with his.

Medium High Nose

A person with a medium but high nose is clever, wily and selfish by nature. He can trick anybody to have his selfish interests served. You can find womanly qualities in him too. Such a person is man outside but woman inside.

Oblique Nose

A person with an oblique nose is not reliable. He may be engaged in things like thievery, deception, flattery and the like. Such a person thinks how to attain maximum by doing no hard work. He can cheat people by living a grand lifestyle or opening a fake company.

Spread Out Nose

Those with a spread out nose are selfish, greedy, with an intention to have their own axe to grind. They can stoop down to any level in order to have their selfish interests served. They are so self-serving that they will salute you until they have some selfish interest to serve; and when their interest is fulfilled, they will disappear into thin air.

Swelled Up Nose

Those with a swelled up nose are often addicted or drunkards. It is hard to tell what they will do the next moment. They have a short temper. They don't listen to others and want their own things to be accepted by others. In addition to anger, they also possess ego and sexual urge.

Dry Nose

Those with such a nose are quiet by nature. They are engaged in their own matters. They also help others whoever seeks it, they don't disappoint anyone.

Depressed Nose

In it, only a tiny nose is visible on the face. It appears to have been crushed by something. Such a person is low on intellect, so he finds himself unable to do anything. He is easily taken in by the sweet talk and deceived, and thinks such a person will help him.

Parrot Nose

A parrot nose means a pretty nose. A person with this type of nose is inclined towards arts and artists. Such people are mostly on high posts. They have no lack of wealth and luxury. They are also opportunistic and refuse to identify a person when their self-interest has been realized.

Pig Nose

Those with a nose like that of a pig are lazy and liar by nature, they criticize others. People with this type of nose like to do petty jobs, they take joy in doing such things.

Eagle Nose

People with such a nose are furious, cruel, heartless, trickster and selfish type of people. Their intellect is not sharp. They pay more attention to trivial aspects. They start to explain things to others while they themselves have not understood them well. They themselves live a life of disorder, yet they teach others how to live a pretty and systematic way of life.

Inflated Nose

Their nose is inflated like a bun. People with such type of nose are fond of eating; they partake of all types of foods with interest. They also like to listen to eulogies sung in their honour. They like to make friends with people of lower strata in the society, so that they might continue to be admired. They also help their friends with money and other things. Due to their help, they are quite popular among people. This popularity is encashed by them during elections.

Shabby Nose

This type of nose is unshapely and looks shabby. People with such type of nose like to wander about, watch movies and have fun. They like to argue with others and trouble them too. It is their habit to argue without any valid reason.

□

10

Know by the Ears

Man listens to any sound by the ears, which are located on the side behind the whiskers between the mouth and head. They project out of the body, and occupy an important place in a man's life. The shape of the ear can be varied, and its characteristics help to identify a person.

Upturned Ears

Those with ears upturned towards the brain are extremely hesitant and suspicious. They can doubt you over any

matter, due to which they lead a very unsystematic way of life.

Short Ears

Those with short ears lack self-confidence and patience. They are timid, cowardly and scared by nature. They are surrounded by a number of fears before they start to do something; consequently, they cease doing a thing even before they have done it. Their family life is disturbed. Their wife flees from them due to their timid and cowardly nature. They work hard, but they lack the courage to advance in life.

Large Ears

If the ears are larger in proportion to the face, they are peevish, lazy and jealous by nature. They are habituated of quarrelling with others and they stop it only when they have got their way. Those with large and broad ears are intelligent, learned and earnest; such people succeed in every enterprise.

Ordinary Ears

People with ears of ordinary size are equipped with a number of good qualities. They do all things after due thought and become expert in any work in no time.

Cascading Ears

Those with hanging ears downward are surrounded by a number of irregularities in life. As they are not punctual, they cannot accomplish work on the given time. Failure seems to accompany them at every step of life. Due to repeated failure, they are subjected to mental disturbance too.

Proportional Ears

Those with this type of ears live a life of struggle. They work hard but fail to get success in it. They are very talkative by nature, due to which they are able to speak their heart out to anybody.

Round Ears

Those with round ears live an orderly and regulated life. They are disciplined and systematic. They are also kind, wealthy, friendly and fortunate.

Square Ears

Very clever people possess this type of ears. They use their cleverness and wickedness to manage resources for themselves for enjoyment.

Stuck Ears

Those who have ears adhered to the body are intelligent, hardworking; they are good artists. They like to live a magnificent life full of luxury and comfort. They are clever, dexterous and wealthy by nature. They love their family members deeply. Their family life is very happy.

Flat Ears

Those with flat ears are farsighted and do everything after due thought. They try to achieve everything on the basis of their hard work. Their family life is quiet satisfied.

Sharp Ears

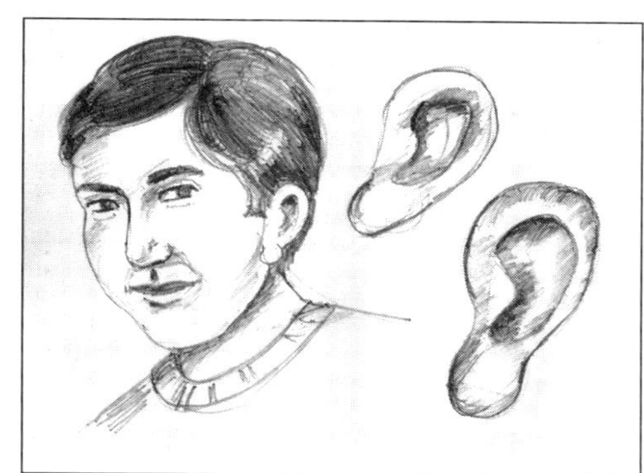

People with such type of ears are adamant, clever, wily and wicked. They are given to determination. They achieve what they once think of.

Monkey Ears

Those with ears like that of a monkey are fully permeated with greed, anger and attachment, which makes their life quite irregular and unsystematic. Owing to these reasons, they fail to get satisfaction in their family life.

Shell-like Ears

A person with ears shaped like a shell is a sex symbol; he is given to excessive sexual urge. He is attached to his wife greatly. Such people are good and noble by nature, but it is difficult to forecast when their mood will undergo a change.

Mouse Ears

A person with small ears like that of a mouse is polite, civilized and kind by nature. His family life sees ups and downs, mixed with good and bad things.

□

11

Know by the Hair

These days, body language is learnt with some specific purpose in mind. Pretty damsels learn it in order to take part in beauty contests so that they can learn how to present their qualities of energy, vigour, efficiency and beauty in an adequate manner.

Hair is the crown of the head. Hair can be of different types. It is on the basis of type of hair that several merits and demerits of an individual can be identified. There is need to pay minute attention to the hair in order to understand a person. Even a tiny negligence in this respect can lead to misunderstanding of his personality.

Soft Hair

Those with soft and pretty hair are simple, soft and quiet by nature. It is in their habit to help others in their need. They grieve when they notice others' grief.

Shiny Hair

Those with shiny and pretty hair are kind, good at heart, noble, patient, attractive, healthy and have other positive qualities. They try to work hard in order to achieve their goals. They have worldly wisdom, and are art-lovers. They take interest in some or the other art.

Thin Hair

Those with thin hair are simple, happy, and they possess positive and beautiful thinking. They are good

at behaviour, patient and cultured. They take interest in creative activities. They are popular among people owing to their good and noble nature. However, they fail to derive advantage out of their popularity right until their end.

Curly Hair

Those with curly hair are masters of an attractive personality. They like to be out of the home, rather than be at home. They like to wander about. Those with curly but stiff hair are peevish and not practical in behaviour. They disobey others, they do what they feel like, and they try to bring others under their influence.

Dry Hair

Those with dry hair are often harsh, furious, adamant and excited by nature. Those with dry but stiff hair are powerful, sturdy and angry. If dry hair is also grey and dark, then the person is egoistic, adamant, and restless. He possesses a poor memory and loves to live life full of lust.

Thick Hair

Those with thick hair are selfish, cruel, heartless and vainglorious. Such people are expert in how to get things done by others. They are wont to quarrel with others and to impress others.

Dark Hair

Those with dark, shiny and attractive hair are reliable, affectionate, kind, honest and loyal. If each strand of hair is thicker, they are powerful and determined. If hair is shiny, it shows aggression in behaviour.

Golden Hair

Only a few people possess golden hair. People with such type of hair are wicked, vainglorious and romantic by nature. They are smart to look at, so they are out to trap girls somehow, but they seldom succeed in this endeavour.

Light Colour Hair

Those with hair of light colour possess multidimensional talent; they have profound insight and friendly. Such people undertake any venture after due thinking, but they lack concentration and patience.

Brown Hair

Those with brown hair are liberal and affectionate. They are true lovers, good friends and do others' good. They mould themselves as per the situation. They have interest in arts. They themselves are good artists too.

Red Hair

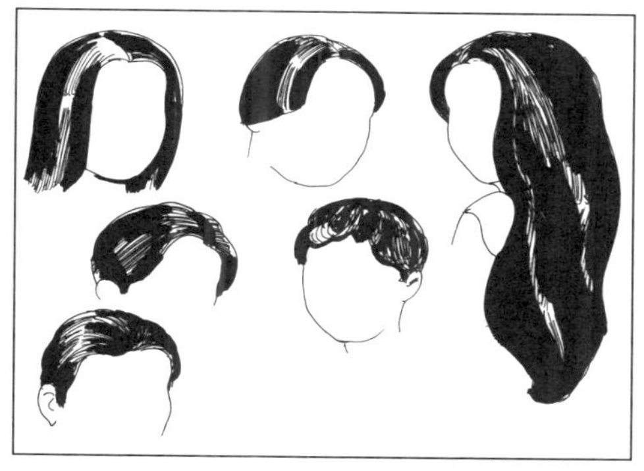

People with red hair possess a quick temper, but they cool down immediately after. Their mood keeps changing from time to time, from sadness to happiness to despair. They are less capable of taking decisions. They are friendly, and have a number of friends.

Short Hair

Those who get their hair trimmed short try to find fault with others in everything. They are autocratic by nature. They have no attachment to music, singing, arts and like things. They are wont to argue with anyone who discusses art with them.

Long Hair

Those with long, shiny and soft hair are sensitive, art-lover and education-lover. They are associated with some art themselves. They always respect the artists.

Adhered Hair

Those who apply oil, lotion or cream on their hair to keep them stuck to the skin, they are impractical, shortsighted and unreliable. They lack the power to think deeply. They can flow with the current. They can trust anybody in no time, and reveal all their secrets, due to which they are often deceived.

Mixed Hair

Those who have knotted mixed hair are prone to laziness, indolence and talkativeness. They waste most of their time in useless things. Such women too waste their time in spreading rumour and are able to do their household work somehow. They lack intellect. If guided, they are able to change their nature too.

Middle Parting Hair

Those who part their hair from the middle, they are courageous who speak clearly. Their thinking is progressive and innovative. Those who part hair from right to left are reliable, kind and affectionate, they don't want to see anybody sorrowful.

Hair Dressed Backward

Those who dress their hair backward are fond of reading books, writing dramas, acting and taking part in other

artistic activities. They like to drown in their own thoughts. They often think purposelessly. They don't like to mix up with others much.

Bun

The women who dress their hair behind into a bun are punctual, efficient in work who abide by the rules. They wish that everybody, whoever comes into their contact, should follow the rules. They get angry at those who don't follow the rules.

Those who tighten their bun are somewhat hard-hearted and selfish. Those who like to put flowers in their bun are romantic, sensitive and emotional, who are prone to trust anybody quickly; they are sometimes deceived due to this nature too.

Keeping Hair Like Men

Those who get their hair dressed like that of men have some manly tendencies and qualities. They think in their hearts to be like men, to fulfil this type of desire, they get their hair dressed like men. They also like to wear manly clothes. Such women are also assertive, who try to prove before men that women are by no means inferior to men.

They command their husbands and children like men. They even adopt harsh or soft behaviour in order to get their say accepted. They don't like to cry or sob like women; they don't try to adopt womanly tricks and glances too. They like to work shoulder to shoulder with men.

Hair to the Front

The women who have a plait of hair to the front are quiet, simple and soft-spoken by nature. They are also intellectual and thoughtful. Those who have plaits on both sides like self-adulation. They are more talkative and friendly too; However, they can say something which hurts deeply.

Mustaches

Mustaches are said to be the pride of men. You can identify a person's personality by his mustaches. Mustaches like that of Hitler show a hard heart.

Short Mustaches

Those with short mustaches are lonesome. Those with short, dense mustaches like bristles of a toothbrush are the ones who like to work like servants. People with short and light mustaches like to show off, often knowingly in order to attract others. They like to be admired. Such people are excessively talkative. They talk without any head or tail, so people keep off them.

Those with short and thin mustaches like to do political and social work. A person with short and adhered mustaches has one thing inside and another outside. Those with very light mustaches possess some womanly qualities. They like to embellish themselves like women. To realize this purpose, they get their mustaches shaved, so that they might look like women.

Long and Inflated Mustaches

Those who keep a long but inflated mustaches are friendly by nature, they like to mingle with people. Those who keep twisting their mustaches by

the fingers, they are proud by nature. They take joy in impressing others. Those with long and dense hair are happy and entertaining. Those who have very long mustaches inclining downwards at the sides are prone to show off. They also like to do something extraordinary. Those who like to change styles of their long mustaches are art-lovers.

Thin Mustaches

Those who keep thin mustaches like a pencil are determined and resolute. They accomplish what they have decided upon once. Those who have sharp mustaches lack self-confidence. They are scared to start a new enterprise out of uncertainty. They are still scared when their work is going on well. They always think that their work can come to a standstill somehow.

Mustaches Inclined Downward

Those with the edges of the mustaches inclining downward are suspicious by nature. They think a hundred times before undertaking a task. They possess a large number of negative thoughts in them, due to which they fail to make optimum use of their talent.

Those with mustaches turned downward are lazy, scared and lonely; they are scared to talk to others. They are scared to meet others in order to conceal what is going on inside them. Those who have a few strands

of hair on the mustaches, they are cruel, heartless and harsh by nature. Such people go to any extent in order to have what they want.

Beard

A person possessing a beautiful, pretty beard is the one who is happy, friendly and intelligent. Those with a light and shabby beard have a nature just opposite to the above. Those who have a soft beard are soft-hearted, simple, quiet and dextrous. Those with thin and light beard have womanly qualities in them, even their body is delicate.

Those who keep their beard well-set are punctual and regular. Those who decorate their beard in different ways are art-lovers, but they are also lazy and extrovert. Those who keep a long beard are quiet and intelligent.

Those who touch their beard repeatedly are careless and angry by nature.

Those who tie their beard with a rubber band are uncivilized and unsocial; they care for neither themselves nor others. Those who spread out their beard are volitional by nature. Those who paint their beard in different colours possess an unstable mind. Those with grey hair, as white as butter, are intelligent and possess a balanced equilibrium.

□

12

Know by the Gait

Everybody has a particular way of walking. It is hard for a person to understand his own gait or walking style, but others can notice him how he walks, and on this basis, they can find out about his nature, disposition, condition and personality. A person coming from far can be identified by the manner of walking whether a man or woman is coming, because each of them has a different gait.

If a person is happy, you can find energy and swiftness in his gait. He walks quickly and takes his steps dexterously. When somebody is annoyed or unhappy, his gait undergoes a transformation. He will walk as if he is carrying a heavy load on his head.

His shoulders will cascade down, and will take steps as if they are made from iron.

Those who swing both hands forward and backward are the ones who wish to attain their goals, and who make efforts to realize their dreams. The people who keep their both hands in the pocket even during summers are rather serious and unrevealing; they don't reveal their secrets and mysteries to others. This type of person also takes interest in bringing insult to others.

Those with a careless and unshapely gait are those who are shabby and rustic by nature. In the same way, those who move thumping their footwear on the ground are uncivilized. Raising dust while walking is the mark of identity of an illiterate and rustic person.

Those who clench their fists while moving arms forward and backward are selfish and self-interested type of people. Those who walk while laughing or talking loudly are selfish and showy type of people. Some people do it to attract others to themselves. Such people look for their selfish interests everywhere. They are little concerned about the gain or loss being caused to others.

Those who throw their hands forcefully while walking are uncivilized and unsocial types of beings. They are not ashamed of anything. They can tell anything to anyone. They can start fighting at the drop of a hat. They don't realize what they are up to. They can pick up a quarrel even with a stranger passerby.

A young girl who walks in a quiet, simple and fascinating manner is simple, quiet and pretty by nature too. Such a girl is engaged with her own matters. The women who walk like models on the ramp are ambitious by nature. They can attract anybody with their fascinating gait. They are ready to do anything for their selfish interests.

Those who walk quickly at one time and slowly at another have unstable type of mind. Those with unequal

distance between different steps can be mentally ill.

Addicted people have a wavering gait. Some people can walk in this manner even without any addiction. They are wicked and wily people; such type of gait is called Shakuni gait, this name has come following the famous wicked character in the Mahabharata. They possess a good general knowledge of almost all subjects; but they employ their mind in the evil things. Those who walk an unbalanced gait lack in self-confidence. They use others in order to realize their goals.

Those who walk with measured steps are intelligent and sharp-minded. Those who meet failure often walk slowly; they don't realize where they are going. Those who kick at things lying on the road have anguish in their hearts against something, and they try to pacify themselves in this way.

Those who occupy more place while walking, they are adamant and staunch. Such people walk while waving their hands left and right, forward and backward. They little care who is walking near them, passersby have to save themselves from them. Such people are vainglorious; they are the victims of superiority complex.

Those who have unshapely gait are unreliable. Those who walk in this manner are also trickster and dishonest. If their neck is bent forward, they can be very evil; it is hard to tell when they can trick others.

Those who move quickly but without swinging their arms, they are professional type of people. They are absorbed in their own work. Those who walk with gap between their feet are timid type of people. If you rebuke such a person, he would lose his equilibrium in no time out of fright.

Some people walk like a turtle. They are lazy, miserly and unreliable. Such people wish that they may get everything without making an effort for it. Those who bend one shoulder to a side, they are opportunistic and selfish type of people. They take joy when they have incited two people to fight with each other.

Those who walk soundlessly, they are intelligent, learned, friendly. They have a broad knowledge. Their disposition is very simple and civilised. Those who walk like a peacock or deer, they are very patient and systematic. They complete their project very carefully and intelligently. They don't like to rely on others for their own jobs.

Those with elephantine gait are serious, intelligent and farsighted. They are very simple by nature. However, if somebody points a finger to them, they will not spare him in any case. Those who walk like a cat are balanced, quiet and friendly type of people. Those who walk like a lion are proud and confident. They always keep their goal before them.

When a person bows down his head and neck into his coat, slips his hands into the coat pockets and bends down while walking, looks up on some occasions only to look down on the ground; such type of a person feels as if he has lost something and he keeps looking for it. If his face manifests feelings of sadness, it simply shows that he is desperate, fatigued or disappointed. He seems to be a worried man because he is not getting optimum success in his enterprise.

If you see a man marching ahead in a hurry with both hands on the hips; swiftness can be gauged from his gait clearly; this type of gait reveals that he is in a hurry to reach his destination. Such a person has abundant energy and possesses special capability to plan for the future.

When you find a person with both hands locked at the back walking with the head a little down, just like a philosopher, you can know that he is deep sunk in some thought or worry. Such a person is prone to sometimes kick a piece of rock lying in the street; and at other time, he may not touch even a piece of paper. Such a person is habitual of considering all aspects of a problem. He keeps telling himself that he should think out all aspects of a problem.

When a person walks with his head held high in all glory while swinging his arms forward and backward, you should know that he is a self-contented man. He likes to live in comfort. When such a person walks, he moves his hands in such a style knowingly and takes his steps in a floundering style, and he does all this to impress others.

□

13

Handshake and Behaviour

Hands have their own language, which can be well understood at the time of a handshake. Coming together of hands is a powerful medium of communication. It is an art to shake hands in order to infuse your views into the other even when you are not acquainted with the other person. When you shake hands

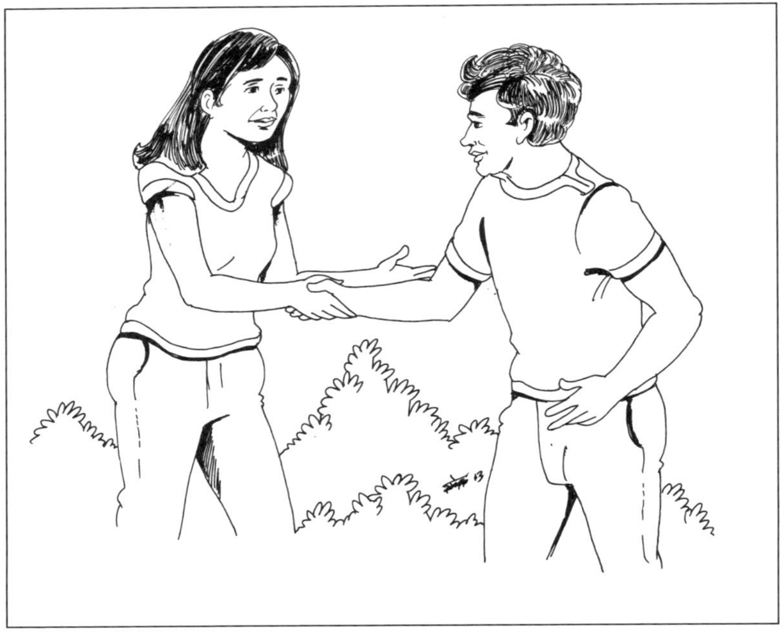

with somebody, you can guess what is going inside him by the manner of his handshake. The manner of handshake reveals a person's personality as well as what is going on in his mind.

The manner, in which people shake hands with others, reveals their personalities. The body language specialist, Tom Kale says that one can read the personality of the other person by the way he shakes hands with someone else. Its style also helps to reveal the personality as well as nature of a man or woman which will help to know more about the person.

It is hard to tell when the custom of handshake started. Research conducted in this field has revealed that handshake was quite in vogue even during the time of Early Man. At that time, when man set out of his cave, he would display his palms in order to tell that he had no weapons with him. With the passage of time, this custom of putting forward palms underwent a transformation. With it, changed many signals and gestures such as empty palms, palms in the air, palm on the heart and the like.

It is also assumed that handshake is the modern form of primitive surrender in which a side laid down arms. At that time, people laid down their arms, moved ahead with the hands extended to the front and then shook hands. During the Roman period, people drew one another to embrace. With the passage of time, this gesture kept changing and finally it culminated into handshake.

There was a time when everybody could not shake hands. There were certain rules and conventions regarding it. The servants could only touch the feet of their masters. The wealthy would not only shake hands but also embrace each other. The nobles had the permission to hold the crown's hand as well as kiss it. Women did not have the right to touch men, nor did men had the right to touch women. Violation of this edict resulted into punishment by caning.

The tradition of handshake prevails all over the world, but it is used in different ways at different places. In France, handshake is undertaken when a guest arrives or leaves. In Germany, people shake their hands only on the arrival of guests. In some African regions, it is considered uncivilized to shake hands.

In the modern age, handshake means welcome. You shake hands with a person when you welcome

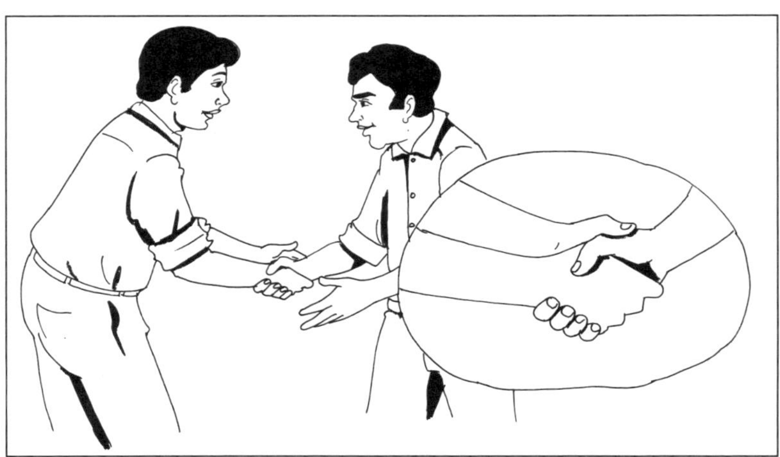

him. When you shake hands, the space between two palms shows liberal attitude, while their touch with each other shows a sense of attachment

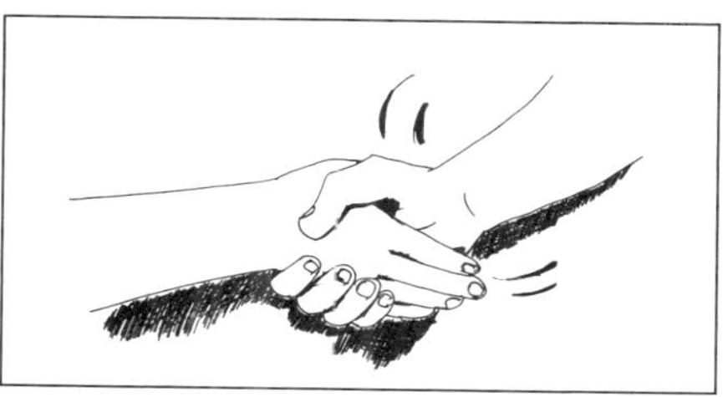

and empathy. As this tradition has assumed global connotations, it is performed at almost all places all over the world. People hail others in order to express their joy.

If a person, while shaking hands, turns the other person's hand downward, it shows that he is trying to prevail over the other person, he is trying to bring him under his control. He turns the opponent's hand downward in order to signify his wish to keep him low like the floor.

People of certain professions often decline to shake hands, such as musicians, artists, surgeons, models using their hands and the like. The reason behind this is that they are egoistic. They belong to such professions in which hands are used optimally, they do so to protect their hands from any harm.

The specialists who study gestures and physical expressions say that the personality of a person with whom you are shaking hands can be revealed by this gesture. Normally we can see that our palms sweat during nervousness. Cold, loose or dead-fish handshake is undertaken only under certain circumstances.

When a person shakes hands in a loose manner, it shows that he is a lazy, desperate and disappointed type of man. When a person shakes hands with a sorrowful heart, his handshake reveals that he is not happy to meet the other person, only he is doing it for formality. If you tell such a person to do something or ask him for some favour, you can be sure that he would not do it; and if at all he does it, he would not do it wholeheartedly. He is shaking hands only to satisfy you, but in fact, he is refusing to do it. The way he shakes hands reveals what is going on inside him.

On the other hand, when somebody shakes hands with you with all the energy and vigour, it becomes evident that he is happy to meet you; and if you tell him something to do, he would try to do it in all earnestness. He will try to do something which will get him success. Such a handshake tells us that the other person is true at his heart.

There is a difference in the ways how energetic and infirm people shake hands. When an energetic person

shakes hands with others, he will do it gloriously and vigorously. You can find his hand full of energy; it starts to fill you with energy when you touch it. On the contrary, when you shake hands with a person of infirm personality, it feels as if you have held a dry stick.

Those who keep their arm straight and stiff while shaking hands, they are respectful and wealthy. It is called men's handshake. When somebody steps ahead to shake hands, it shows that he is welcoming you heartily.

When a person does not offer his hand when you extend your hand to him, it shows that he is a selfish, self-serving and egoistic type of man.

When a person places one hand on the back side of your palm, it shows that he wants to take you under his control. He wishes that you should follow what he wants you to do.

If a person covers your hand during a handshake, it tells that he is a person of a clean heart, and he can do anything for your sake. It also shows his reliability and honesty. It is called glove handshake. But keep in mind that when somebody shakes hands with you in such manner in the first meeting itself, it shows that he is dishonest, selfish and trickster, he is prone to deceive you at any moment, and you should keep off from such a person.

Those who shake hands loosely are moody and lazy by nature. Their manner of shaking hands reveals that they are not satisfied with you. They are sure in their mind that their ambitions cannot be realized through you.

Those who press your hand during a handshake, it shows that the other person is egoistic, furious,

disobedient, assertive and staunch, who are not ready to listen to others. Those who shake hands repeatedly, or those who tap your hands softly during a handshake, they are somewhat selfish by nature. If a female does this, you can take her to be willing, and such a woman can do anything for the sake of her selfish interests.

If a woman draws you near her while shaking hands, it reveals that she is scared of something and she needs security. This scare can be unknown or imaginary too. A woman who shakes hands energetically or who kisses the hand is a happy and pure-at-heart woman.

A woman who shakes hands with more than one man at the same time, she is supposed to have more than one boy friend. If a woman has dirty, rough nails and you do not want to shake hands due to this fact, such a woman is rustic, work-shirker, unclean and adamant. A woman who only touches fingers and does not shake hands well, she is egoistic and selfish by nature.

Some people shake hands in a very loose or cold manner. Their hands are like a dead fish. Such people are very lethargic by nature, who find no joy in meeting any type of people in the world. They think that everything in the world is useless. They do not trust anyone in the world.

Those who bow to the front a little are reliable, hardworking and honest. If they balance their body weight on one leg, it tells that he can do anything for your sake. If a person holds the fingers tightly during a handshake, he is vigorous, energetic and happy by nature. Those who press tips of the fingers, they are impractical, rustic or unsystematic type of person. Those who hold only the tips for a handshake, they lack self-confidence and are timid.

When a person pulls another during a handshake, it can reveal two things. Firstly, he can display attachment and is being influenced by the other person, so he draws him near him.

Secondly, he is trying to impress the other person. He wishes to say : "Come near me and do what I wish to tell you."

Those who shake hands with both hands are vigorous, reliable and earnest type of people. Everything they do is clear and clean. They are ready to do anything for the people they love.

Those who cross hands to shake both hands, they are stupid, selfish and useless fellows; they care for neither themselves nor others. Those who cross hands for a handshake and then rotate round, such people are simple to look at; but they are, in fact, one thing outside and other thing inside. They are very dishonest and wily. At every moment in life, they have one or the other scheme up their mind how to deceive the other person.

Those who hold the elbow of the other person before a handshake, they are simple, quiet and cooperative people. They hold the elbow in order to reveal their approval or cooperation. Those who hold the upper arm and not elbow, they try to reveal their sentiments in a clearer manner. Those who hold the other person's arms, do so in a bid to express their sympathy. They mean to say that they will cooperate, so the other person should not worry.

If a person holds both arms together and shakes them forcefully, it shows that he wants you greatly, and is expressing his love and attachment for you.

□

14
Know by Gestures

People rub their hands after they have lost everything. In winters, you will find people rubbing their hands together in order to evade cold. A fiancée starts to rub her hands when her fiancé is late to come and starts to walk up and down the room.

The fist raised upwards is an aggressive posture, that is, a person is energetic and vigorous, or is excited against the system. When the fist is to the front, it can mean an offensive posture, it is necessary for you to save yourself from the attack that can ensue at any time.

When a person removes his glasses and starts to clean them, it shows that he is finding it difficult to take some decision; his mind is clouded by a number of things, but he is not able to arrive at the right decision.

When somebody is angry, the wrinkles of his forehead are stiffened. When he shows teeth, it shows that he is aggressive.

Modern science is yet to develop a machine which could tell or display what is going inside the mind. However, scientists, psychologists and sociologists all over the world have been studying man's different types of physical gestures and expressions in order to study the mind and their effect inside them. This helps to know more about a person's nature, disposition, character, lifestyle, personality and the like.

It will be interesting to know that our forefathers had found out much about man's nature, disposition, conduct and character by the movements which occur outwardly and inwardly. This topic finds mention in our ancient treatises, physiognomy and astronomy. Reading body language is a difficult task. It is very important to employ and use very carefully so that true meanings could be gauged out, because body language undergoes a change as per the time and place, and the same gesture could mean different things in different contexts.

The basic manner of mutual conversation has remained uniform ever since the ancient times, such as shaking hands, nodding head, waving hands, silent approval by eyes, expressing acceptance and the like, which are done by different organs of the body. The bodily gestures continue to emit signals. Much can be understood about the other person through his hair and hairstyle, face, smile, walking style, manner of speaking and the like. All these things can also reveal the mood of a person at a particular time.

When somebody bites lips, it shows the stress that is prevailing within him. When somebody raises eyebrows, it shows anger or aggression. When somebody rubs his eyes, he is not able to trust what he is seeing; and when somebody rubs behind the ear, it shows that he is not in a position to take a decision. If somebody deviates his eyes while talking, he either is telling a lie or is trying to conceal something. Shaking hands shows nervousness. Biting nails shows that the person is confused or scared. Dropped shoulders show that the person is in financial difficulty.

It is an art to read different gestures of body language. It requires some hard work, but then you start understanding it well. In order to help you know more about different gestures, I shall describe different gestures and what they mean.

Reading Gestures

Bus station, railway station, airport, park and such places are convenient places to study different gestures of people. These are the places where you will find a large number of people, and it helps to notice large number of gestures.

If you look at people carefully, you will find that their gaits or walking styles are different; they all walk in their unique style. The expressions of one person are different from those of the others. A person appears joyous while another appears to be sorrowful or stressed.

The passengers who meet their relatives and friends, they appear to be happy. Their gait is swift and joyful. When a person, who is waiting for his relatives or friends, rises up on his toes to look here and there in search for his loved one, it shows his attachment for the person he is waiting upon.

If you gaze at a person over a long period of time, it will help to read his feelings. Those who come to receive their guests or friends, they appear to be happy. If a person is leaving for a long duration, his face reveals sorrow. Those who keep going on tours regularly, their faces are filled with boredom, and they do not like to travel. If a person is going to a distant place in search of work, his face shows stress with the feeling of uncertainty of the unknown.

Sometimes a person pinches his palm to reveal uncertainty of his mind which is scared and confused. This reveals that they have landed at a new place and it seems to them quite unbelievable. You will find a person

cursing himself when the train is late, while he needs it urgently. Then there are others who have landed in your town for the first time and they are full of curiosity.

You will find a person sitting on a bench with one leg crossed over the other and hands near their body with the straight back. Such people are habitual travellers. They are confident and they know what time the train or plane will come. They keep their ears to the announcements in order to know the latest situation. You will also find some people who will lock their fingers of both hands and tap them with the thumbs. Those who do this are nervous, and they are trying to camouflage their nervousness by this gesture.

If you study people talking in a telephone booth or over the mobile phone, you can find out who the person is and whom he is talking to. If you find a well-dressed man talking on phone carefully, or paying all his attention to what is being told to him, or is responding in a relaxed manner to what all things are being told to him, it reveals that he is a salesman. If you consider all gestures and body stances together, you will know that he certainly a salesman who is busy talking to his customer or client. He talks to his customer as if he is right before him.

When a person drops his body loose and talks bowing ahead a little, he is sure to talk to his old friend.

If a person is standing against the wall and is talking in a hushed manner that others cannot hear, he is certainly in conversation with his fiancée. Those who shout at a public place over the phone, they are illiterate, rustic or not-so-well-mannered people. They little care for the inconvenience they cause to others, they have only their own purpose in mind.

Reading Facial Expressions

Body language should be learnt by all people. This is a psychological language, which you can use at different places to get the different purposes served. The well-known psychologist, Jane Tampliton Ting says that a salesman should be a good student of body language, only then he can be an effective salesman.

In this connection, Jane has written a book for salesmen. He has described different gestures in this book. If a client has lowered his eyes and has turned his head the other way, the salesman should take it that he is

not taking interest in the product. However, if the client appears to be delighted, and you do not think it is artificial smile, if his chin is to the front, then you can be sure that he is considering your product. If the client looks at the salesman constantly for a few seconds, and is smiling at the same time, and his smile reaches right up to his nose, you can be sure that he has made up his mind to buy the product. If his face pervades with a broad smile and there is a feeling of curiosity on the face, you can know that he is about to buy the product.

A good learner of body language ought to know the emotions and sentiments that emerge on the face. It is necessary to notice such emotions carefully. But you cannot do this if you directly look into his face or eyes. For this, you have to keep an eye over his gestures stealthily. You will have to ensure that his work is not interrupted, nor should he guess that somebody is observing him.

If you observe a person, you should make sure that the person under study is not able to know this fact, else artificial gestures would envelop his face. A bus station, railway station, park, sea beach, mall, airport, market, seminar, party and meeting can be a perfect place to study others without letting the subject know of it.

Gestures and Signals

During conversation, some people can place their one hand on the shoulder of the other person. When a person holds the other's hand by his right hand, and places his left hand on his shoulder, it shows mutual closeness; it shows that two close friends are meeting.

When you study gestures, you should also observe the emotional changes that take place along with them. Under a certain situation, the conduct of a person can immediately change from openness into reserved attitude. If you leave aside a few exceptions, man often communicates his emotions and mental conditions through non-verbal cues. These gestures are full of sentimentality.

If you want to study the personality of a person, you should observe what he is saying and how he is telling it, and the gestures that go with it. Later, study his individual gestures and signals how they harmonise into the whole. If you study a person at different occasions, such as in business or social contacts, you can form a certain opinion about him.

If you want to know how open a person is to you, how devoted he is to you, how impressed he is by you and the like, just study his gestures, observe his facial expressions and body movements, and it will reveal lot of things about him.

When a person puts his open hands ahead, it shows his honesty, truthfulness and openness. When a person is angry or unhappy, he raises his both hands to his chest and says: "What do you want from me after all?"

When a person is perplexed, he raises and drops his shoulders, and raises his palms upward in order to display his disability. You might not have noticed this gesture in daily life, but this is a common practice in films to show a troubled character. Film artists often adopt this gesture in order to express their sentiments.

When a child secures good marks, he presents himself proudly by keeping both hands to the front. He is swelled up with pride and joy. When he is marred by some suspicion or confusion, he feels guilty, he hides his hands behind his back or in the pocket.

In a Meeting

In a business meeting, it is often seen that some members remove their coats.

Keeping the coat open displays self-confidence of a person. Specialists studied the videos of business meetings and minutely observed the gestures of different participants. They found that the members with unbuttoned coats were more positive and supportive towards a new agreement, while those with buttoned-up coats were not so, they displayed stress.

In a business meeting, if a person has buttoned up or zipped his jacket, has his hands locked, is the one

- Sense of insecurity : biting nails, biting pen or pencil, trying to keep away, backing out, sweating on face.
- Lie : deviating face or eyes, not contacting eyes, changing track of talks, rubbing ground with toes.
- Confusion : tapping head, rubbing behind the ear or on the nose.
- Aggression : kicking things with feet, punching the palm, throwing things.
- Fury : pulling hair, red face, red eyes, crying and shouting.
- Approval : low eyes, coming near, bright face, vigorous body.
- Non-approval : keeping off contact, turning away, making faces, enlarging eyes.
- Attachment : embracing, shaking hands, kissing face, tapping head.
- Nervousness : shaking legs, trembling hands or feet, sweating on hands or face, feeling thirsty, dry throat, stammering.
- Vigour : being happy, jumping about, laughing openly, dancing, crying and shouting.
- Joy : clapping hands, laughing, enjoying, raising hands to dance.

□

15
Know by Sleeping Posture

A large part of man's life passes in thinking about others and understanding them, still he fails to know and understand others. There are numerous small things which can be observed to know about a person's character and personality, such small things include the way in which a person sits, stands, walks, talks, or even how he sleeps. A person sleeps in different ways as per his nature. You can know the personality of a person by the way he sleeps.

Curled Up Posture

Some people turn to a side and curl up legs right up to the stomach. Those who sleep in this way are envious

and selfish. They get angry quite too soon, due to which other people want to keep away from them.

Supine with Hands under Head

Those who lie down in a supine posture with hands spread out like to live a comfortable life, they are also spendthrift. They undertake different types of measures in order to look pretty. They are good at talking and can forget other things while talking.

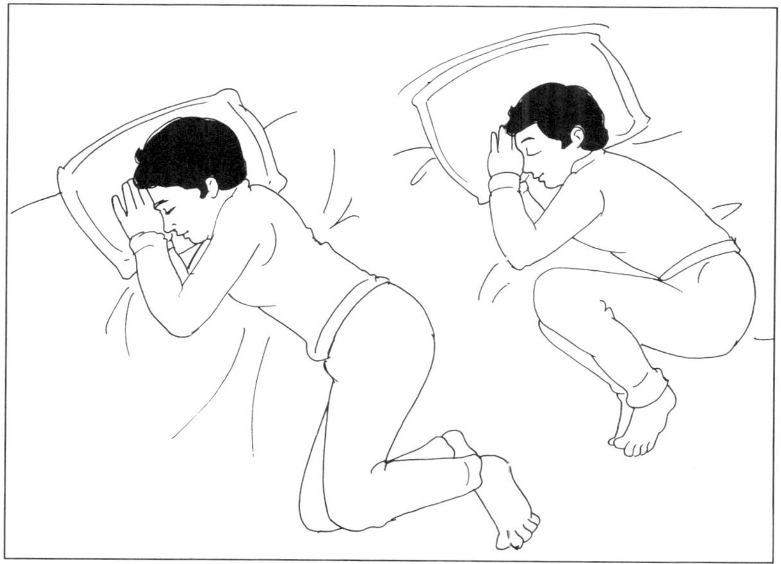

Those who fold their hands under the head while sleeping in a supine position, they are intelligent; they maintain friendly relations with all people, they have a large number of friends too. They take some time before they start to like someone. Those who sleep in this posture are good managers, but don't like anyone so easily. Maybe they are choosy than others.

Turn Posture

If the sleeping posture of a person is such that he has turned to a side with his head at the edge of the pillow with legs straight, then such a person is fortunate. Those who sleep on the side are replete with self-confidence, and they get success in all the fields.

Bundle Posture

Some people turn their legs right up to their chests or shoulders. This shows loneliness or disappointment and lack of self-confidence. Due to lack of self-confidence and trust in themselves, they take time or hesitate to take a decision quite often.

Those who sleep in a bundle posture with legs folded up to the stomach, like a foetus in the womb, they possess a delicate and emotional heart. Anything can hurt them so easily, and they can become upset by anything. Such people give preference to their needs before those of the others.

Folded Knee Posture

Those who fold one leg up to the stomach are hasty by nature. They are wont to complain at every other thing, and they can cry or shout at anything under the sun. These people are also prone to become disappointed, desperate and stressed so easily.

If a person folds both knees a little to sleep on the side, he is an honest and affectionate man. He is also sentimental, polite and civilized. Such a person never harms other people intentionally. They are noble at heart and people like them too.

Those who sleep in this posture maintain friendly terms with most people, because they notice good things in others, and overlook their shortcomings. Few people possess this type of qualities. When the time comes, they are harsh on themselves and start to criticize themselves. If they happen to commit a mistake, they become quite perplexed, and keep thinking over it for several days.

Holdall

Some people act like a holdall, that is, they cover themselves right from toe to head. Those who sleep in this manner possess dual personalities. They appear to be harsh and determined before others, but in fact, they are quite hesitant, sentimental and introvert.

Prone Posture

Those who sleep on their stomach, with the face downward are self-centred; they possess narrow views. They wish that others should understand their needs and help them. Those who sleep in this way possess a very balanced intellect; they are cold-minded. Such people are quite adamant on what they think, and don't accept others' contention so easily. They command others to fulfil their needs, but they find it difficult to adjust with others. Despite this fact, they are popular people.

Supine Posture with Crossed Leg

Those who sleep on their back with legs crossed over each other, they are a little proud and egoistic, and they are happy with themselves. They find it hard to accept any change whatsoever.

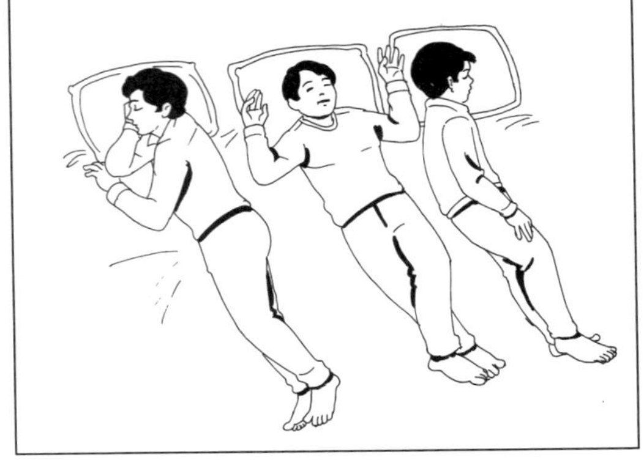

They think that everything should happen as they want it to. They are always lost in their past experiences. They like to be alone. They are liberal and tolerant by nature.

Those who cross their hands under the head, such people are energetic and understanding, but have some irrational views. They want to look after their families well, but don't know how to go about it.

□

Clean Dress

Those who wear a clean and well-ironed dress, they are disciplined, energetic, vigorous and ambitious by nature. A clean dress also tells about their self-confidence. Such men are not very enthusiastic about friendship. They seldom get angry, but if they happen to be angry, then they become very aggressive.

Disorderly Dress

Those who wear a disorderly dress are unsystematic and pessimistic people, who think about only negative or dark aspects of life, and are demotivated all the time. They are fatigued and lack ambitions in life. Such men often like to do tasteless and riskless jobs.

Dark Dress

The men who wear a dark colour dress are self-confident and self-dependent. They are open by nature. They are not that much energetic, and can share their personal matters with only few people.

Irregular Dress Patterns

The men who wear dresses with irregular patterns are liberal and friendly. They are critical about others. They are efficient in their work, but they are quickly bored up of tasteless things.

Striped Dress

The men who like to wear striped dresses are happy-go-lucky by nature. Often their family members complain against them as they don't do their work ably and efficiently. They are normally efficient, and like to enjoy themselves after they have finished their work.

Dot Printed Dress

The men who wear a dress with tiny dots are hesitant and disturbed people who can indulge in self-adulation for the sake of hiding their shortcomings. Such men often remain in their wives' control.

Socks

Those who wear tight socks are energetic by nature. They accumulate and save on their energy. They work carefully, and do not hesitate to undertake new experiments in life. They get success in life owing to their self-confidence and willpower.

Those men who wear loose, folded or dirty socks are careless and unsystematic type of people. They are often anxious for their own comforts. They are not able to maintain balance between home and occupation, and are often troubled and perplexed.

The lipstick used on the lip can be observed to know the personality of a woman.

If a woman applies lipstick in a circular shape, it tells that she is friendly by nature, she remains happy, and she likes openness.

If the shape of lipstick is deep oblique, it shows the aggression or force of sentiment brewing inside her mind. Such a woman has ambitions to do something in life, and she also encourages others surrounding her too. She possesses vigour and energy for life, and is enthusiastic and optimistic. She is also romantic by nature.

Some women apply lipstick in a uniform way. Such women are honest by nature, and they have equal feelings for all people. Such women possess a delicate heart and like simplicity. If lipstick becomes pointed on the sides, it shows a balanced and enterprising way of life.

Shoes Reveal Personality

The experts of body language are of the opinion that the personality of a person can be known by new or old shoes. If a person's shoe has torn from the inside, it shows that he is leading a life of discontentment. He wishes to emerge from this dissatisfaction, but lacks courage to do so.

If there is a hole in the sole of the shoe, it shows that he is habituated of talking in a measured way, he takes due consideration before deciding upon anything. Often, such people are very miserly; however, they are prone to spend money like water when a suitable opportunity comes.

The people whose shoes have rubbed or torn at the edge on the outside, experts say that they are happy, joyful, lively, clean-spoken, romantic and sweet by nature. Such people can be made happy by a little flattery. They are scholarly too.

If the outer edge has completely torn, it shows that he is happy-go-lucky and carefree by nature. He is worried about nothing in life. He is spendthrift too. Such people fail to keep their wives happy, and discord is common in their marital life.

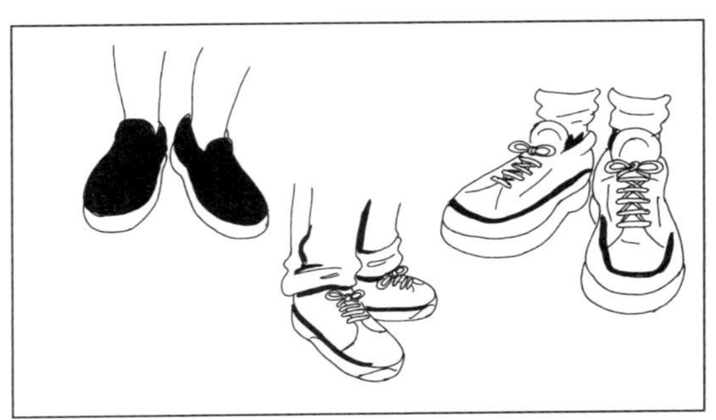

Those who have fully used up shoes, they are the ones who are drowned deep in anxiety. They struggle

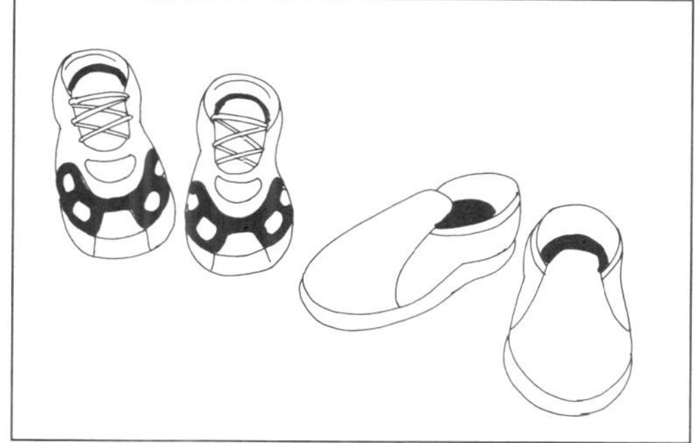

at all times, but success eludes them. They are peevish by nature. They are always confronting difficulties and troubles.

Those who get stars or nails driven into their soles, they are miserly by nature. They bargain a lot when they are out shopping. They can rub the heels on the road while walking. They waste their shoes and at the same time, waste their life as well. Such people are quite unfortunate and penurious.

Those whose fingers leave a mark on the shoes are aggressive and quarrelsome by nature. They are also suspicious. Those who shine their shoes well possess a fine personality and are good at behaviour. Those who wear clean and shiny shoes are careful to their work and efficient. They are also sensitive. Such men like to help others too.

Those who don't pay attention to the cleanliness of their shoes are careless and indolent by nature. They wish for success in life, but hesitate to make efforts and perseverance that are needed for it. They depend on their luck rather than hard work to become wealthy.

Dirty Nails

Nails show beauty, therefore, one should pay attention to them. Nails can reveal the secrets of any person and his personality can be gauged through their observation. It can be easily guessed whether a person is careless or conscious towards his task. This guess depends on the extent of his cleanliness of nails.

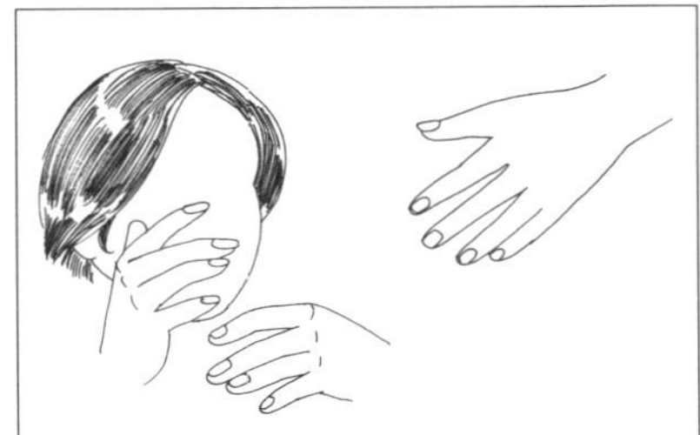

If nails are trimmed short, clean and without polish, it means the person is practical and does his work on time. If he spends a lot of money in making nails look good, then such a person is extravagant by nature.

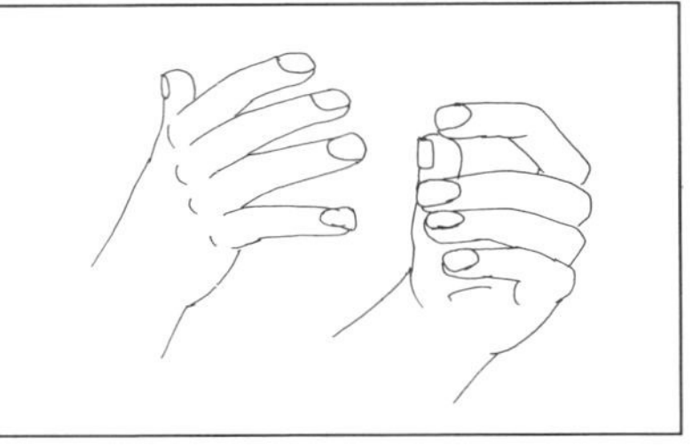

If nails are not clean and are grown shabbily, and they are dirty, it shows that he is careless and lazy by nature.

Simple Dress

Those who like to wear a simple dress are simple and conventional people; they are straight and noble by nature. They are not very energetic, but they are full of confidence. They are capable of moulding themselves in any situation they confront.